GOTHIC NOVELS

GOTHIC NOVELS

Advisory Editor:
Dr. Sir Devendra P. Varma

THE

PASSIONS

Volume 1

CHARLOTTE DACRE

("ROSA MATILDA")

New Foreword by Sandra Knight-Roth

New Introduction by Devendra P. Varma

ARNO PRESS

A New York Times Company

New York—1974

135768

Reprint Edition 1974 by Arno Press Inc.

Special Contents Copyright © 1974
   by Devendra P. Varma

Gothic Novels II
ISBN for complete set: 0-405-06011-4
See last pages of this volume for titles.

Manufactured in the United States of America

———◆———

Library of Congress Cataloging in Publication Data

Dacre, Charlotte, b. 1782.
    The passions.

    (Gothic novels II)
    Reprint of the 1811 ed. printed for T. Cadell and
W. Davies, London.
    I. Title. II. Series.
PZ3.D123Pas4 [PR4525.D119]   823'.7   73-22762
ISBN 0-405-06013-0

For
Frank H. Cunningham
—historian and archaeologist—
who read for me the hieroglyphic on
the tomb of Tutankhamen:
*"To take the name of the Dead
Is to bring them back to Life."*

Foreword

Charlotte Dacre's novels briskly circulated from the shelves of the circulating-libraries and were avidly seized upon by the readers of the day. Her fast-moving stories invariably unfold exciting adventures in exotic climes. The Italian landscape, the Venetian and Neapolitan settings, were considered ideal for romance, especially for deep and passionate attachment between man and woman. In the England of the eighteenth century, reading, speaking and singing in Italian were considered as indications of a cultured upbringing, and a visit to Italy was an indispensable must on the Grand Tour. To the English mind, the warm Italian climate and its sunny skies chimed admirably with the passionate character of its inhabitants, and such a trait was ideally suited to the tumultuous events in a Gothic novel. This attitude is manifest enough in each of Miss Dacre's fictional works.

Miss Dacre's style evinces a subtle voluptuous quality which is distinctly her own. Cast in a different mould than those of her precursors, her heroines do not exhibit any elegance or artificiality of diction, nor coy daintiness of mien, nor any inveterate ingenuousness of character. Even her supernatural events are not explained away. Although her characters have a melodramatic turn, the major ones are notably well-drawn. They are human and have human feelings. They are faced with choices and lured by temptations. They make decisions and very often they make mistakes. Consequently they suffer because of their errors. They are far from being idealized figures.

Love and marriage have always been, and probably always will remain, important to women. When Miss Dacre wrote her novels, women did not have the freedom they have today, and a proper choice of a husband was imperative. Morality was also of utmost importance, and if a maiden once lost her virginity she could no longer expect to enter into a prestigious matrimony. It is possible that Charlotte Dacre experienced some of the difficulties she herself describes. The dilemmas of her heroines could very well have been ones which she or her contemporaries had faced. In this respect her works mark a step forward in the development of feminine characterization in the novel. Unlike Pamela, Clarissa, Emily or Antonia, Miss Dacre's women are not one-dimensional beings concerned with propriety or taste. They think, feel and reason.

Gothic lineaments can be traced in the works of Poe and Hawthorne, and the psychological interest in the mind of the criminal has been explored further by Dickens. Mrs. Radcliffe contributed a deeply-felt passion for the cyclorama of nature, providing a base from which the Romantic poetry of Wordsworth, Keats and Byron could take off. Charlotte Dacre, on the other hand, took pains to create more down-to-earth, individualized characters, and brought some psychological credibility to the personnel of Gothic fiction. Despite the tight-lipped disapproval of Victorian society, Charlotte Dacre's colourful novels continued to be read through the nineteenth century, proving perhaps that forbidden fruit always tastes the sweetest.

Toronto,
Canada

Sandra Knight-Roth

Introduction

Far be't from me unkindly to upbraid
The lovely ROSA'S prose in masquerade,
Whose strains, the faithful echoes of her mind,
Leave wondering comprehension far behind.
—English Bards and Scotch Reviewers, 1809.

Miss Dacre's final novel, *The Passions**, published in 1811, was offered for one guinea. Deviating from the style of her previous works, *The Passions* conforms to the epistolary mode in the tradition of Samuel Richardson. Ninety-two letters of various length and content are exchanged between Count Weimar and Baron Rozendorf, or between Rozendorf and Darlowitz, before the author suddenly streams into a prose conclusion. Some epistles narrate specific incidents while others are protracted philosophical introspections on life, love or morals.

The *Critical Review* of December 1811 was rather harsh:

> The inflated extravagance of diction, which deforms Rosa Matilda's novel of *The Passions*, deducts very much from the interest which her work would otherwise have excited. The effect of her talents, for talents she undoubtedly possesses, is impaired by the repulsive affectation of her style.

Dacre's ornate language, florid style, and melodramatic incidents must not be assailed, however. Traditional Gothic machination is once again in evidence: Julia, the victimised heroine, and Appollonia, her merciless pursuer; excessive

---

*For further discussion of Charlotte Dacre's novels, see the Arno Press editions of *Confessions of the Nun of St. Omer, Zofloya; or The Moor,* and *The Libertine.*

ix

emotions and ill-fated amours leading to disaster; the suicide of
Darlowitz; Julia's desire to enter a convent, and her
subsequent derangement; all these are reminiscent of "Monk"
Lewis. But the sublime is incorporated more effectively in *The
Passions* than in Miss Dacre's previous works, while there
subsists greater interaction between the characters and nature.
Whereas the actors lapse into highly embellished dialogues, the
letters of Julia and Darlowitz exhibit perception and
imagination, while the concluding scenes of the novel are
undeniably moving.

The story opens with the imperious Appollonia Zulmer, a
handsome young widowed Countess in the environs of Vienna.
The narrative recounts the tale of her frantic love for the
fascinating Count Weimar who fails to reciprocate her passion.
Appollonia's infatuation then changes into obdurate hate.
Maintaining her external composure and friendliness, she sets a
complicated machinery of revenge in motion. The Count
departs for Switzerland for a change of scene and climate.

Dacre displays a fine insight into the psychology of love.
According to her, man is never vindictive against the woman
he has once loved. If she cannot reward his passion, she may
cause pain but does not exasperate him. He will cherish his
grief in secret, because man is more proud and has more
fortitude than woman. He will quietly endure the lacerations of
his soul, but will always entertain some tenderness for the
female he has once loved. Without any bitterness against her,
he will rejoice in an opportunity to render her service, for she
has a claim on his heart, having once stirred it with exciting
sensations. Woman, on the other hand, nurses vengeance. Hate
springs from the moment she ceases to love, and her tenderness
gives way to outraged vanity. Between these two extremes of
passion, she hardly knows any other alternative.

During his sojourn in Switzerland, Count Weimar falls in
love and marries Julia. Appollonia is seemingly cordial and
gradually wins Julia's friendship and confidence. Typical of
Gothic romance, Dacre's characters are personifications either
of consummate goodness or unmitigated evil. Julia is soft,

gentle, honest; she is loving and kind, and leans on her husband for guidance. In contrast, Appollonia is cold, scheming, deceitful and vicious, and pledges to educate Julia in the ways of the world.

After many twists and turns in the story, Darlowitz, another lover, overcome by mounting passion, begs Julia to elope with him. She, incapable of handling the situation, decides upon a flight from both her husband and lover. Julia's lengthy confession to Weimar explaining how she "sinned beyond repair" has echoes from Shakespeare:

> Light heavy on me, shame, disease and want!
> whistle around me ye winds of heaven! beat me to
> the earth, ye storms, let me grovel on the dust—

Darlowitz commits suicide by shooting himself. After a great deal of hardship, Julia finally arrives in Switzerland and seeks shelter with an impoverished mountaineer and his family. She longs to enter a convent in Zurich to perform penance for her past. Appollonia is delighted with Julia's tale of anguish and misery. Meanwhile, the shock of horrible revelations deranges Julia.

The whole tale is a series of misadventures and planned revenges for unrequited love. Weimar disguises himself to visit Julia. Her distractions are Ophelia-like: her features are sunk and wan, yet her cheeks are tinged with a carnation glow; her eyes dart a painful brilliance, "her hair hung partly loose and partly bound up with yellow and withered leaves," and in her hand she bears a withered branch which she waves to and fro.

Although never violent, she loves to wander when the weather is stormy, sunk into a profound melancholy, and spends days by the window looking vacantly in the direction of Lintz. With many memories surging up in her troubled brain, she determines to visit her husband's dwelling once again, and one dark evening in a gathering storm she flees in her diaphanous night-gown. This particular scene is exceedingly poignant: we hear the rustling of the wind amid the leafless branches of the trees, when like a frightened deer she bounds forward with a palpitating heart, afraid to look behind. The dreary and desolate landscape of an unvarying waste of snow gleams faint in the dewy light of the pale moonbeams. The arrowy sleet dissolves upon her breast, still glowing with the fever of her heart's despair! A piercing blast strikes against her loose tresses and fiercely howls round her defenceless form! Her bleeding feet, sore and torn, stumble forward leaving traces of trickling blood. At the doorstep of her former home, just as she is about to knock feebly for admittance, her faltering steps and failing strength give way and she collapses as the heavy snowflakes wind a soft pall over her dead body. The following morning Weimar discovers his wife's corpse as he prepares to take an early walk.

The pathos of the closing scenes is truly impressive and remarkable and calls to mind a scene from a later work—George Eliot's *Silas Marner*—in which the linen-weaver discovers Molly's snow-covered corpse.

The Passions appeared on a list of new publications in *The Quarterly Review* for May 1811. But *The Critical Review* for September 1811 paid more attention to this novel and provided a brief summary along with some critical comments on the author's inflated, extravagant style of language, powers of invention and talents for description. The reviewer pointed out that all the *dramatis personae* were either madmen or madwomen, and the diction was bombastic. The unbridled passion of overstrained unlawful love had a ring of destiny and fatality. The faults of this romance were pointed out: the cause of all the misery was attributed to Appollonia's revenge; yet the misfortunes of Julia seemed to stem substantially from the unbridled passions of Darlowitz, over whom Appollonia could exert no control. The pride of Weimar was wholly unaccountable and unnatural. *The Critical Review* rounded off by saying that

> there is much unnecessary distress, which ancient critics disapprove of in tragedy in whose sentiments we moderns participate.

Yet despite several glaring defects the story has a considerable charm. The scene is laid first in Vienna, afterwards in Italy and parts of Germany, and the passions which Rosa Matilda has attempted to exemplify are revenge, hatred, jealousy, love and pride. Besides striking situations, certain spectacular scenes stand out prominently: Mondovi disguised as a postillion driving a coach into the Black Forest, descending and dragging forth his victim and piercing her with deadly wounds; Rozendorf and his servants alarmed by the shrieks of the wretched woman, rushing to the scene, rescuing her, and, having disarmed the brigands, lodging her in a wayside inn where she expires in excruciating agony. The character of Pietro Mondovi, a shadowy figure, who flits in and out of the story with sinister schemes, is truly a shade of Radcliffe's Schedoni.

Miss Dacre presents ample proof of her classical erudition by continuous references to Ixion, Prometheus, and fabled Hell. She colours her narrative with subjectivity, personality and some intimacy. She reveals the workings of the human mind when influenced by emotions and environment, and surely, her type of writing precedes and points out the later developments of the interior monologue or stream-of-consciousness technique.

Charlotte Dacre brought out an anthology of her poems, *Hours of Solitude,* in two volumes, almost simultaneously with her first novel. This collection, along with those fugitive pieces that appeared at intervals in *The Morning Post,* gives us an insight into her poetic genius. Published in 1805, it contained an engraved portrait of the author by Buck. *The British Critic* of March 1806 remarked on "lovely Rosa" that

> she has an attractive person, as well as a poetical pen; and she takes care to tell the public, in a short advertisement, that she is still only three and twenty.

A number of verses are addressed to a gentleman, presumably

Miss Dacre's lover. She expatiates upon all the qualities and characteristics of a true lover. Her poem, "To Him Who Says He Loves," is followed by "The Answer," written by a gentleman named George Skeene who affirms that Rosa's physical beauty reflects her intellect, and confesses that he is her captive because of her "superior worth." This, furthermore, raises an interesting query. A critic, while pointing to the poetical merits and paintings of nature, suggested that many poems in the second volume were actually written by Azor, a lover of Rosa Matilda. It would be interesting for a scholar to explore the vicissitudes of her career; undoubtedly she must have been like one of her tormented heroines, a bright-eyed fugitive damsel haunted by gothic dreams!

Montague Summers has described Miss Dacre as an author who "revelled in vapid lyricism." Her lyrical effusions are lively and musical, sprinkled with incidental philosophy but never deeply intellectual.

The popularity of her anthology cannot be refuted, because a second edition was called for within seven months. In a brief note to the public, Miss Dacre confessed that most of the verses were penned at the age of three-and-twenty. *The Edinburgh Review or Critical Journal,* April-July 1805, had announced the publication, and so had *The Scot's Magazine and Edinburgh Literary Miscellany* for July 1805, but neither offered any critical comments. But *The British Critic* of March 1806, said that "the poems chiefly relate to love, of which poor Rosa seems to have felt all the vicissitudes. That she had also poetical feelings in her hours of solitude, we are far from attempting to deny." Commending her poetic effusions, the critic "leaves the poetess to her muses and her lovers." She had undoubtedly experienced all the successive phases of the emotion of love: joy, despair, pleasure, sorrow and passion. She expounds this favourite theme with all its trials, tribulations and temptations; she carefully discriminates between the baseness of passions and the enchantments of true affection.

The *Hours of Solitude* contains thirty-seven poems. The

second volume also includes an appendix of seventeen selections penned by Miss Dacre in her early teens, poems that reveal the youth and naiveté of the author.

Miss Dacre sometimes practiced a style similar to MacPherson's *Ossian,* in her sensitive observations and imaginative descriptions presented in pieces such as "Fog," "Will-O-Wisp" and "Wind." A number of gothic elements gleam through some of the lines. The twenty-six stanzas of "The Skeleton Priest; or The Marriage of Death" are replete with skulls, blood and ghosts, reminiscent of "Alonzo the Brave and the Fair Imogene."

Widely read, Miss Dacre had a true taste for the romantic. "The Lass of Fair Wone" is important for the German influence of Bürger, and "Moorish Combat" reflects the British interest in foreign names and exotic settings. In "The Maid of Cashmere," the interest in the exotic reappears, and "Thorbiorgia; or The Icelandic Witch" indicates that Miss Dacre had a fascination for the Nordic legends current in England during her time.

Charlotte Dacre enjoyed considerable renown in the field of popular music of her day. *The Morning Post* of June 22, 1805 advertised "some beautiful compositions in a Collection of Airs written by ROSA MATILDA." The avidity with which this production was sought by music lovers fully endorses the merit of the composer. Her musical fame lingered throughout her productive years. *The Morning Post* of March 12, 1806 bestowed the following praise: "Among the most admired songs of the present day, are those which have been lately produced by the elegant and classical pen of ROSA MATILDA," and pronounced the verdict that these were "confessedly the best poetical productions that have for many years been set to music."

It is not in the choice of incidents alone that Charlotte Dacre purloined material for her pages, but also in sentiment, characterisation and scenic description. Her occasional philosophic musings and moral counselling do not seem to intrude upon the tapestry of her tales. We pause only momentarily to reflect upon these infrequent observations before plunging again into the labyrinth of action and adventure.

The local colour of Italy is manifest in the settings of her romances and in the titles of some of her poems. Most exciting episodes invariably occur against the exotic backdrop of Venice and Naples. The warm climate and southern skies reflect the tumultuous deeds of passionate characters. Arieni is an Italian noble and Cazire luxuriates in sunny Italy in *The Confessions of the Nun of St. Omer*; the setting of *Zofloya* is Venice, while the adventures of *The Libertine* are recorded in the environs of Naples. Julia and Weimar in *The Passions* undertake an excursion to Italy to feast on its art and architecture.

While some of her characters become melodramatic or weak, the major ones are well delineated: Cazire, Victoria, Gabrielle, Julia or Appollonia—all leave a lasting impression. This success in character painting may be attributed to her keen powers of observation and experience, or even to mere feminine intuition. Faced with choices and temptations the creatures are trapped in the vortex of their errors.

Although her novels did not rise to that prestigious immortality of Mrs. Radcliffe's works, Miss Dacre may undoubtedly be considered a radiant star in her own domain of the gothic galaxy. If the gothic novelists attempt to strike a union between our spiritual curiosities and venial terrors and mediate between the world of mystery and reality, Miss Dacre was precisely motivated by these principles. She plumbed the intricate depths of the human mind and listened with compassion to the agonised cry of the human soul. Combining melodrama with sentiment and romance, she bequeathed to the gothic novel a new tone of psychological realism.

Dalhousie University
Nova Scotia

Devendra P. Varma

Select Bibliography

I. GENERAL
(on Gothic romance)

Birkhead, Edith, *The Tale of Terror.* 1921

Railo, Eino, *The Haunted Castle.* 1927

Tompkins, J.M.S., *The Popular Novel in England (1770-1800).* 1932

Praz, Mario, *The Romantic Agony.* 1933

Summers, Montague, *The Gothic Quest.* 1938

Varma, Devendra P., *The Gothic Flame.* 1957

Lévy, Maurice, *Le Roman "Gothique" Anglais (1764-1824).* 1969

II. Charlotte Dacre's works:

Hours of Solitude. 2 vols. London, 1805

The Confessions of the Nun of St. Omer. 3 vols. London. 1805

Zofloya; or The Moor. 3 vols. London. 1806

The Libertine. 4 vols. London. 1807

The Passions. 4 vols. London. 1811

III. SPECIAL

Chesser, Eustace. "Introduction" *Shelley and Zastrozzi: Self-Revelation of a Neurotic.* Gregg Press. London. 1965

Hughes, A.M.D., "Shelley's Zastrozzi and St. Irvyne," *Modern Language Review.* XII (1912)

Knight-Roth, Sandra. *Charlotte Dacre and the Gothic Tradition.* (unpublished Dalhousie thesis) 1972

Summers, Montague. "Byron's Lovely Rosa," in *Essays in Petto.* Fortune Press. 1928

——. "Introduction," to *Zofloya; or The Moor.* Fortune Press. 1928

Varma, Devendra P. "Introduction" to *The Confessions of the Nun of St. Omer.* Arno Press. 1972

——. "Introduction" to *Zofloya; or The Moor.* Arno Press. 1974

——. "Introduction" to *The Libertine.* Arno Press. 1974

THE PASSIONS.

In Four Volumes.

By *ROSA MATILDA,*

AUTHOR OF

HOURS OF SOLITUDE; THE NUN; ZOFLOYA;

LIBERTINE, &c.

VOL. I.

Hell has no fury, like a woman scorn'd!

_____

LONDON:

PRINTED FOR T. CADELL, AND W. DAVIES,

STRAND.

1811.

THE PASSIONS.

LETTER I.

COUNT WIEMAR TO BARON ROZENDORF.

Switzerland.

AT length, my dear Rozendorf, I have reached these delightful solitudes; I breathe at ease—my soul soars, as it were, above the weaknesses of my nature, and its immateriality is no longer matter of metaphysical doubt in my mind. Great God! it is only when gazing on the sublime and terrible that we can conceive something of thine ineffable grandeur—it is when ascending the steepy mountain, while, at each step, new worlds seem to rise on our view; it is

when gazing from the dizzying height
o'er an immeasurable expanse of earth
and waters, of hills, piled on each other,
and towering to the clouds—of summits
covered with eternal snows—of icy plains
seeming stretched in mid air, and glis-
tening like diamonds to the powerless
sun-beam, or like immense burning mir-
rors reflecting it—of barren heights and
cultivated vallies—of the loud rushing
cataract, fiercely foaming and dashing
with wild velocity down the unfathomable
abyss, dazzling the sight, confounding
and overpowering the sense. Yes! these
are the scenes where the Godhead is best
adored; where his wondrous magnifi-
cence and power is not left to the feeble
grasp of human comprehension, but
where it is displayed, spread out before
the eyes, and reaches the mind and heart,
not by conception merely, but sublime
reality.—What is the prayer of the priest?
What are his feeble images of God's im-

mensity ? what are they compared to scenes like these, which speak more deeply, more powerfully to the soul in a single moment than the most eloquent dissertation. Oh ! when on these proud heights, how is my ethereal essence elevated and purified ; it ascends beyond the clouds— it catches for an instant a glimpse of eternity, it trembles, awe-struck, at Heaven's gate; I am no longer a mortal.— How frivolous, how vain, how contemptible, appear the cares of the world, the nothings of life !—how could I ever be swayed by likings or antipathies ? how could I ever feel pleasure or pain at the various follies which make up the sum of existence ? How could I ever appoint and propose, and look forward to years ? how could I dream of the future, or feel interested in the past or the present? My whole existence seems wound up in a single moment of ecstasy, of enthusiasm ; I feel almost beyond the verge of common humanity; I am sensible that I breathe, that I exist, yet the inspiration of my soul encompasses me around, and lifts me above this earth. But now the mists of evening begin to gather—the day was as soaring youth, when all is glorious and beautiful, and fervid imagination embellishes the prospect—the evening, is age; when all is chilled and dim, when the mind losing the stimulus of external objects, the imagination too becomes less ardent; the vast variety of sublime images which have transported me out of myself, retire, mingle, and gradually blend into gigantic outline—the delirium of the soul ceases by degrees, I descend again to earth, but bearing an impression in my breast which will aggrandize and dignify my nature; I vow, in my heart, to become worthy of having been created by so great a God.

This morning was surely the most delightful that rose upon man; the snowy heights, sparkling to the sun, dazzled the eye with a glare of light and brilliancy; it was impossible to remain in bed and behold this prospect unmoved—I hastened to breathe at large the pure keen air. With a stick that I have, armed with a spike of iron at the point, I ascend the mountains with the expertness of a native. I made use of it to gain a height, where I promised myself a prospect that would recompense me for my trouble. When I had ascended about half way up the mountain, I saw a little to the right a man, who appeared to be asleep; I approached him, and with caution, for I perceived that he was slumbering on the brink of a precipice, his head reclined on a fragment of rock; a cap of chamois skin partially covered his face; part of his body appeared clothed with the same; his great coat was thrown loosely over him, and a rifle gun lay beside him.

I instantly knew the sleeper for a chamois hunter, the desperate free-booter of the Alps. I gently awakened him.

"Friend," said I, " you have slumbered too long." He started up.

" I was dreaming," said he, "that a chamois was leading me a most unconscionable chase."

"Had you started in your sleep," said I, pointing to the precipice—" had you moved but an inch"—

" Oh! as for that," said he, " there was no danger, I slept too soundly; I had a hard chase last night: will you have some breakfast ? ' added he, offering me some brandy from a stone bottle that hung at his girdle.

I declined his offer, and he drank himself; then, breaking a piece of hard black bread in two, he again made a tender to me, which I again refused.

"Well, then," said he, "farewel; I've no time to spend in compliments."

"Which way do you go, friend?" inquired I.

."I know not," he answered; "wherever my prey appears I shall follow," and he looked round with a piercing glance.

The race of the hunter, though he was still a young man, bore the marks of age; it was haggard, lean, and deeply indented; but his eyes, though sunk, were ferocious and wild, his dark brows were knit, and his bold features were those of a hardened warrior, scorning danger.

" Why," said I, " do you lead this life ?"

" I like it," he replied.

" How can you like an existence so hazardous, when the dreadful perils you encounter make each moment precarious ?"

" Life is always precarious," he answered; " what matter whether a man dies by falling down a precipice, or in his bed?"

" Have you a family ?"

" To be sure I have."

" Then if you were to perish they must starve."

" My hunting supports them."

" But could you not occupy yourself, with equal advantage, in some less dangerous employ ?"

" I told you before I liked this; its danger is its charm to me; hardship makes pleasure sweet; those who live always at home find no comfort in it; after I have been for forty-eight hours, perhaps as long again, traversing regions of ice, exposed to wind and snow; after I have been scrambling up mountains, breaking precipices, encountering the savage wolf, or fierce Alpine eagle, to rescue my prey from them, is it no zest to my enjoyment of home, think you, when I return loaded, after all these fatigues, with the young chamois on my shoulder? when I can present the beautiful skin to my wife, and regale my young ones with the flesh for supper? Farewel! the agitation of life is its greatest charm; could you become a chamois hunter you would always remain so " So saying, he bounded up the side of the mountain; he gained the summit before I could have got half way; then, looking eagerly round, he descended with equal velocity, rose again on an eminence, plunged down again, and, buried among the mountains, I soon lost sight of him.

What a life to lead! Yet they are insatiably fond of it, and would rather miserably perish in its dangers, than think of foregoing it. All the answers and observations of this hunter to me, were truly illustrative of the hardened ferocity of their character, their contempt of danger, and even of death; nothing can appal them; they pursue their prey on the brink of the most dangerous precipices; a sort of magic seems to impel them—they rush onward—their very fearlessness is their protection; and amply recompensed are they if they conquer their self-created foe, the innocent chamois. The creature knows man for its destroyer, and instinctively avoids him; seeing itself on the point of being taken, it meditates revenge; it flies to the most dangerous spots; it menaces, but vainly defies him on the steep and elevated ice; near the rushing torrent, or on the edge of the abyss, it aims to precipitate him to destruction who would destroy him. But, vainly still—the hunter braves all; no threatened ill renders the path inaccessible to his determined footsteps; even the rightful and native inhabitant, nay, sovereign of the mountains, is compelled to yield to this human intruder and predator. The chamois is a most elegant and beautiful animal; my fancy likens it to the gazelle of the mountains of Arabia, to which the eastern poets so often compare their mistresses; the slenderness and delicacy of its form, its timidity, its eyes, so proud, so wild, so wandering, the graceful loftiness of its port, all render the comparison most happy, and perfectly in unison with the tender and romantic expression of their ideas. But the hunter is insensible to the charms of the chamois, and thinks only of its value.

I am delighted with the inhabitants of Switzerland : with the utmost simplicity of manners, they combine a refinement of idea, and a degree of native genius, which seems at first surprising. Many of them are acquainted with the best authors, ancient and modern, and a tinge of philosophy runs through their character. The rudest mountaineer among them is not ignorant; it is nothing uncommon to see a herdsman with a volume of Voltaire or Rosseau in his hand. They are universally benevolent, kind-hearted, and hospitable; their women are handsome, modest, and reserved. I do not think I shall very soon quit a spot where I appear to tread more proudly; where, in the midst of these primitive people of the vast solitudes which surround them, I feel more independent, and seem to breathe more freely than in the busy world.

To mix again in the scenes I have lately quitted, would at this juncture be an effort of which I am incapable. What frivolity prevails in society; how uninteresting the men,—how full of vanity the women! I protest to thee, I would not for the treasures of the east undergo another year such as the last I spent at Vienna. I appeared in a light the most detestable to myself, because of the predicament into which I was thrown; did I not seem as a subtle deceiver! a betrayer of woman! Thou knowest the hateful business to which I allude. Never was a man more the victim of misconception and misrepresentation. I never entertained an idea the least serious of the

Countess Apollonia Zulmer. I thought her fair, lively, engaging; but my heart was never affected by her. Scrupulously, rigidly, and with the utmost anxiety, have I examined every sentiment, every emotion of my mind, respecting her, and every part of my conduct towards her. I can find nothing like the semblance of love in the one, nor in the tenor of the other aught she could construe as such. But that her subsequent conduct inspired me with a real esteem for her character, such as I had not conceived her capable of exciting, I might certainly have attributed design to her throughout the piece; it should seem as though she wished (by pretending to believe me seriously inclined towards her) to force me into an alliance with her. Could the most fastidious delicacy have hesitated how to act? Should I bind myself for life to a woman I had never loved, or professed to love, merely because she chose

to misconstrue attentions which I would
have paid to any other female, equally
accomplished, and doing me the honour
to appear gratified by those attentions?
I should have done her an injustice in not
discovering her error to her, for could I
ever have made her happy, had I even
married her from a delusive species of
false delicacy. Yet how odious, how
painful the explanation I was doomed to
give; how wounding to her—how dis-
tressing to me—still I went through the
task—the task which truth and honour
imperiously demanded of me to perform.
Certainly from that hour she rose in my
estimation. How fine her conduct, how
admirable the softness, the dignity, with
which she bore an explanation, of all
others the most mortifying to female feelings. So powerfully did she win on me,
so much did she interest me, that, seized
with a sort of tender pity for her, I was
almost tempted to retract, and sacrifice

myself in the chance of giving her happiness. Fortunately I restrained this impulse of an ardent sensibility; how deeply, how incessantly should I have repented it, but she acquired a claim on me, which will never be obliterated; my love she never possessed; but my friendship, my esteem, my regret, these I cannot withhold from her: may she be happy as she merits.

Still I must acknowledge to thee, this unpleasant occurrence was the efficient cause of driving me from Vienna. I shuddered at the thought of meeting Appollonia; I should have read reproach in every look: but if tender, then daggers would have penetrated to my heart. I avoided her therefore; yet to avoid her, how cruel. In the eyes of every other woman, I saw, or fancied I saw, indignation at my conduct, and the cause of Appollonia seemed espoused by all her sex. In those of the men I conceived an illiberal exultation, an unworthy triumph, that she who had so often disdained and rejected others, was mortified in her turn. I almost dreaded to hear some horrid congratulation burst from their lips; yet how wild, how imaginary these terrors, since the secret of Appollonia was confined to herself and me. No human being surmised aught of what had passed between us; no one could suppose a particular attachment towards me, from a woman who was alike to all.

Had I, by the general eye, been viewed as intending to become her husband; had her preference for me been obvious and remarkable, or my attentions to her borne a distinguishing character; had the public opinion, in short, considered us destined for each other, I should have concluded my conduct must have given foundation for the idea, and I should have felt myself bound in honour to have espoused her; nay, even now, were this thought to obtrude itself on my mind, I would quit these sublime solitudes, and, like the victim for sacrifice, lay my head on the altar; but I believe thou knowest thy friend too well to suspect he could ever voluntarily wed a woman whose deportment was equal to the multitude.

Chagrined and disgusted as I have been, I must, nevertheless, do justice to the Countess Zulmer. I repeat that she has shone forth with a brilliancy unexpected: since this trial she has displayed a delicacy and sensibility I never believed her possessed of—perhaps, had she always appeared equally beautiful in my eyes, I might have loved her.

After all I cannot imagine the occurrence of a more painful circumstance in man's life, than the inspiring a charming woman with a passion which he feels it impossible to return ; it is an involuntary crime, lessening you (I was going to say) in your own estimation : you feel as if you were really guilty, and so you are, inasmuch as you give pain, though you do not do it willingly, and it is this conviction of the pain you inflict, that gives you a feeling of guilt—you are disposed secretly to arraign yourself—your conduct—your manner—your very looks—each, and all, must have been guilty, each must have tended to mislead, to involve in error, and to produce misconception. Are you not accountable then ? Should you not make every reparation ? Ah ! what idea is this ? I am distracted. Rozendorf, tell me, am I bound to do this ? is this idea which glances through my brain founded in justice ? Oh ! Heaven ! say but yes, and make a wretch of me for ever—for if you say it, it shall be done.

View the case with your cool philosophic eye, and tell me truly; spare me not if you think I have acted wrong; and if I ought to——I can proceed no farther, I shrink with horror from this idea, conjured up by a scrupulous inquiring mind; I wait for your opinion as for my fiat; till I receive it I torment myself with doubt, and my examinations of myself are productive only of increased perplexity.

LETTER II.

BARON ROZENDORF TO COUNT WIEMAR.

Vienna.

ONE of ideas too highly refined—of sensibility too acute, should not hastily form a judgment of himself; but should submit, as thou hast done, my Wiemar, the powerful workings of his soul, to a friend unbiassed and dispassionate, that cooler reason may temper the ardour of a generous and enthusiastic nature.

Thus, then, I answer thee. In having acted as thou hast, thou hast acted wisely and well; away then with thy morbid doubts, and the scruples of an overstrained conscience; what has come to thee, my Wiemar? how is thy mind alternately the theatre of the sublime emotions and the most irrational fantasms? Canst thou, seriously, for an instant, admit the belief that thou shouldst have conducted thyself differently in the matter to which thou alludest? What madness is this—what an outrage on reason and morality: to bind yourself by an irrevocable vow, and thus become *perjured* in *promising* to love one whom neither your heart nor mind approves. Be assured you would soon have repented your supposed sacrifice to honour and generosity, and romantic refinement. You would never have made happy the fair Appollonia Zulmer; you would not, after all, have had even that consolation: her nature is so opposite to yours; your dispositions so absolutely contrasted; your ideas so dissimilar, that your conscience may be perfectly at rest from the apprehension, in not having wedded her, that you have debarred her of any happiness within your power to have conferred on her.

With your refined, perhaps too elevated
ideas of what woman *should* be, your existence with the Countess Zulmer would
have been a life of torment. She cannot
breathe out of the warm meridian of gal-
lantry, and universal admiration; think
me not unjustly severe, for I know her,
when I say that the love of one man, nay
of a man ardent and enthusiastic as yourself, would make her no compensation
for the adulation of the crowd. Good
Heaven what would have been your state?
struck with horror and dismay at threatened disgrace, perhaps you might, at
first, have essayed remonstrance or
reproach. But the Countess Zulmer is
of a proud irascible nature; married early
in life to an old man, a stranger to controul, and soon released from the little
check she might have endured, she would
either have laughed at, or, perhaps, been
offended with your anxiety, and to show
you she would not be restrained, have

rushed into wilder dissipation, and have displayed more levity than ever. Conceive what a situation this for you, with your lively feelings and keen susceptibility. I can imagine for you only distraction or suicide.

Never more then, my friend, let me hear a word of regret from you on this subject, unless it be for having permitted yourself to entertain a serious thought on such a woman as Appollonia Zulmer. Banish her wholly from your mind, let your fine reason regain its wonted energy, and suffer not a fastidious spirit of refinement, a nervous sensibility, to get the better of you. Be assured the most scrupulous honor could. never require of you to sacrifice your judgment and truth, to the caprice, (or at least, if you will not admit the term) to the unwished, uncourted preference of a vain woman, who could never appreciate you.

No one has ever dared to cast a breath on the name of a Rozendorf; yet, I swear to thee, by my unblemished honor, that under similar circumstances, I should have adopted the conduct I commend in thee; nor would such conduct have ever occasioned, for an instant, an uneasy sensation in my mind, excepting, indeed, that. I must inevitably have felt a regret at having inspired sentiments I was incapable of participating; but no doubt as to the propriety and justice of the course I had pursued.

True philosophy is superior to the refinements of fancy; and, when it is accompanied with a sound understanding, and a virtuous heart, it seldom errs in its judgments or definitions. I shall consider it a strong proof of the influence my opinions and ideas possess over you, if, in your answer to this, you tell me your

mind is satisfied and convinced, and your
heart at rest.

LETTER III.

COUNT WIEMAR TO BARON ROZENDORF.

Switzerland.

YES, my dear Rozendorf, I am convinced; your friendship has an influence over my soul, which your strong
reason aids and confirms. I will no
longer deliver myself up to irrational fantasms, as you properly term them. You
judge for me as I ought to have judged
for myself. In wedding Appollonia Zulmer, I clearly perceive I should have
done not only myself, but her injustice
likewise, for I feel with you a conviction,

I could not have rendered her happy. How widely different her character from what I look for in a wife. The Countess Zulmer wants simplicity, if I may so express myself; assured of her wit and beauty, she does not endeavour gently to steal into the heart, but attacks it by storm, as able generals strive to carry all by a *coup de main*. Sensible of her power in conversation, whatever the topic, she takes a part, and enters freely; she obtains admiration, astonishment—but not love. Tenderness can be attracted only by tenderness: fearless, regardless of prejudice, an ardent spirit and daring intellect, she discusses opinions, combats errors, exposes systems, detects folly; in each and all she appears great; in every part of her character, full of power. Her fierce and penetrating eyes seem to look into the heart, with a glance so quick, so piercing, that other eyes are unable to meet them, and are cast down, as with a feeling of conscious guilt. Soaring, and eccentric in her flights, she leaves her wondering sex far behind, who gape and stare after her as at a portentous sign in the heavens; she is admired, imitated—and, when she descends from her altitudes, at humble distance followed.

No doubt there are men, to whom the fire and talent of Appollonia Zulmer would be irresistibly fascinating; there are wild romantic characters, who, adoring bold female genius, and a decided original mode of thinking, would imagine themselves supremely blest in her possession; there are philosophers, too, who, disdaining the softer female virtues, admire such only as partake a masculine cast, who consider boldness the test of intellect, and gentleness of folly; who deem freedom grace, and delicate reserve fastidiousness. To such as these would Appollonia appear a star of the first magnitude. Whether, on nearer inspection, through the telescope of marriage, the luminary would seem equally brilliant, is matter at least of doubt.

Certain philosophers, pretending to decry the prejudices of men, contend for the equality of woman.

" We allow them no intellect," say they, " yet expect from them the great qualities of forbearance and fortitude, and attach blame to them when they err; yet how unjust is it to expect proper conduct, to praise or to blame those whom we will allow no judgment to direct. They are not our equals, we say, yet we demand of them masculine virtues."

Thus setting out with a false hypothesis, they of course deduce wrong inferences. Man is not so irrational as to deny to woman judgment or discrimination, nor' yet so perfectly absurd, as to consider them on an equality with himself; for that they are *not*, I believe to be more or less the general opinion of man, though some few, for the purpose of gaining favour with the sex, or from the vanity of wishing to appear above prejudice, assert the contrary.

To these wretched sophists it is owing that such characters as Appollonia Zulmer presume boldly to exhibit themselves; certain of having their admirers, their purpose is gained, for admiration is all they wish, or covet to inspire : they are above the weakness of desiring to be loved. I do not, however, obstinately assert my idea of woman to be the correct standard; I can judge only of what is pleasing to myself. As an ornament for the drawing-room, as full of animation, wit, and grace, I admire Appollonia; but for the cabinet she is unfit. Yet, though

I desire something different for the companion of my life, I believe her to possess a heart so excellent, and principles so sound, that I would not hesitate to introduce either a wife or sister to her society. Behold my picture of a perfect woman:—chaste simplicity, retiring charms—diffidence, modesty, reserve; tender sensibility, yet strong reason; elegant genius, but no eccentric flights; a due estimation of the dignity of the female character, without fastidiousness; a heart, formed for love—but to love only *one*, to seek after marriage no pleasure beyond the sphere of her duty, or the wish of her husband; to be ever, under every ill, his tender consoler, not an imperious reprover; to have no passion, or excess in aught, but *love for him*. Ah! I had better never marry, for where could I ever meet with a woman to my wish—with a second Amelia. Oh! Rozendorf, is not the wife of our friend a concentration of every benign female virtue, grace, and perfection? Most charming of her sex! had she but a sister that resembled her, and who could love me, blessed might I be on this earth. Vain wish! my Rozendorf: waiting for an Amelia, thou and I might ever remain single.

It should seem as if the generality of the sex must be at once dull in intellect, and destitute of beauty, to reconcile them to the dedication of their lives for their husband and children, and to the routine of domestic duties; but here is a woman, at once beautiful and of exquisite mental endowments, cheerfully withdrawing from the world's idle gaze, and devoting herself entirely to the happiness and good of her family. Oh! rare excellence! that can dignify, that can deck, that can brightly illumine the tranquil honourable path of domestic duty, by other women considered so tame and so unsplendid.

Transcendent Amelia! lovely is thy career, and full of glory. 'Tis true, indeed, the vain adulation of the crowd, the buzz of empty admiration, the gaze, the whisper, do not attend upon thy footsteps, but thy way is a track of light reaching to the skies. Mortals do not follow thee, but angels look down and approve. In the midst of society thou art as a brilliant luminary, shedding resplendent rays around ; the centre of thine own circle—the meridian of thy day ! What could the world offer to an elevated soul like thine? how despicable to thee their frivolity ! Thy sacred duties gracefully engage thee ; and, when there is remission from the more active ones, thy fine talents are employed to give entertainment and delight to thy *husband*, to add to the improvement of thy *children*, and to increase still farther the rich treasures of thy own cultivated mind.

'Tis said that perfect happiness is not the lot of man. Not certainly happiness in a religious sense, which teaches that nothing earthly should constitute the perfect happiness of the soul, lest thus it might become too much detached from Heaven; but what alloy, I would ask, to the highest state of bliss mortals may be permitted to enjoy here below, could be experienced with such a woman as Amelia? -Surely, the possession of a creature like her, must be to have an angel shedding benign influence over one! refining, purifying, and exalting him, with whom she holds communion: I feel my ideas harmonized in discoursing of her; I have no longer any unpleasantness or bitterness in my soul—such is the power of virtue. I can behold the heavenly prospects around me with increased delight; my mind, torn heretofore, (I confess it to thee) by harrassing doubts, snatched long moments from my enjoyment of the beauties of nature. Now, I can gaze, and my breast ascends at the views of the vast universe, as it appears stretched out beneath my feet : I long again to climb those frowning rocks—to pause on the edge of the precipice—to hang with pleasing horror over its vast abyss, while my soul involuntarily shudders at the idea, that I am hovering on the brink of eternity !—that a movement of my will alone lies between me and it, and that a single step decides my destiny.

How truly Longinus has observed, that sublimity is in the terrible. How my soul ascends to the vast Creator, in the midst of these awful scenes ! I am transported out of myself; I feel capable of the grandest efforts. Virtue, heroism, is no exertion, power is mine; I could become a Cæsar or an Alexander ! What do their achievements appear to my grasp ? I could outdo them all ! Oh ! this enthusiasm of the soul, bordering, perhaps, on madness ; while we contemplate the stupendous works of nature, how does it exalt man, lifting him, as it were, above his native sphere, and impressing on his mind the deep indelible conviction of a future, nobler state of existence. Couldst thou, my Rozendorf, behold the prospect which lies before me, while writing to thee, thou wouldst deem me neither mad nor extravagant. Is it madness or extravagance for the heart to feel boundless enthusiasm, while I behold boundless wonder ? Then, may I be a madman ever, rather than the tame spiritless clod, who, traversing these sublime scenes—who, contemplating them, should feel his breast dilate with no rapturous emotion, no overpowering admiration of Omnipotence, but should remain in the midst of them unmoved, and uninspired.

'Tis now evening; a dim light begins to prevent me from seeing objects distinctly—this indistinctness, too, is a character of the sublime: the clouds rest on the highest mountains, and their heads, thus enveloped, seem to touch heaven. The mind's eye now and then catches a glance of some mysterious form—imagination pursues it till sense almost totters, and the idea becomes lost. A blue vapour ascends from the lakes like the smoke of subterranean fire; as it rises, the most grotesque shapes and fantastic illusions are combined, and disappear. The dimness increases, the sides of the hills are covered with a white mist, they seem as distant clouds; various rude projections are marked by darker shades, on which the eye resting for a time, fancy grows superstitious, and forms them into huge giants, which appear moving towards us. Here and there a leafless pine, waving with the wind on the dizzy moun-

tain top, resembles some thin ghost bending in mid-air, and beckoning from its
dreamy height.

Such, Rozendorf, are the delusions of
twilight and distance. The realities of
the scene it is not for a pen such as mine
to describe; it should be coolly done,
and that I cannot: I can paint to thee
only in inadequate colours, some of the
vast and various impressions made on my
mind, through the medium of my imagination, or the wild exaggerations of my
fancy; to form a judgment, to be enraptured, thou shouldst be on the spot—
I am too much a creature of feeling and
emotion to be methodical or regular in
my descriptions. While I am writing to
thee, a sweetly solemn air, to which the
lyre of Orpheus could give no added effect, breaks on my ear!—'tis the tender
rans de vaches; its melancholy notes fill
my soul with troubled pleasure, but on

the Swiss it acts with too powerful an impression, frequently dissolving them in tears, or exciting in them the wildest enthusiasm.—Adieu! I begin to feel its increasing influence—a seducing languor steals o'er my senses, tears rush to my eyes, and undefined emotions crowd on my heart. I must leave thee—I long to ramble among those shadowy mists to detect the illusions of fancy, perhaps to imagine new. The invigorating breeze blows freshly on my face through my opened casement, as if to hasten me forth. I inhale at once fragrance and health, and at each breath I experience an increase of physical and mental elasticity. My soul feels refreshed, my mind enlightened, and a grateful sensation diffuses itself throughout my being; in the midst of these scenes my bosom glows with a delicious ecstacy.— Once more, dear friend, adieu!—Friendship and gratitude are not the least warm of the sentiments I love to cherish.

LETTER IV.

THE COUNTESS APPOLLONIA ZULMER TO MADAME DE HAUTVILLE.

Vienna.

HE has gone ! he has fled !—Could you believe it ? Alas, it is but too true !— Fatal passion ! whither hast thou hurried me causing me to forget at once my pride, my dignity, and character. Oh ! my dear preceptress, I blush to confess, even to you, that I acknowledged to the seducer of my soul, the love with which he had inspired it, which drove me mad ! I threw myself on his mercy—he spurned me !——

Oh ! what are the bugbears of anti-quity, the punishments of the damned in their fabled hell? What are the tortures of Tantalus, the labours of Sisiphus, the miseries of Ixion, the agonies of Prometheus; what are they all, compared to the new species of suffering devised by my evil genius for me? which, could I impart to the gloomy monarch of those subterraneous abodes, he would exult in an addition to his power of tormenting. Oh! how I writhe! how inadequate the utmost stretch of imagination, how poor the extravagance of fable, in inventing degrees of torture, or of depicting them; how feeble, compared to an hour of the *real* unvisionary horrors which rack *my* soul, and convulse my reason! What is bodily anguish? what are the pangs which flesh can endure? Is it not the mind alone that can truly suffer? Is it not the soul which is the seat of sensation?

Oh! for ten thousand scourges, applied at once—for the stings of knotted scorpions—for any species of corporeal suffering, that for a single instant might divert to it the superior and unspeakable agony of my soul—that for a single instant the one might be swallowed up in the other.—But, no, it may not be; I am sadly free from physical pain—all, all is soul, the nerve of mind.

You think me mad! I believe I am; but if I am not now, I have been.—Appollonia rejected!—the love of Appollonia spurned!—Is it not enough to turn a brain, such as mine? My love, and my pride at once so outraged—for I loved the traitor—Yes! I loved, and he disdained me.———I must lay down my pen * Though the hour was past midnight, I rushed into my garden, fearless of consequences—what are consequences to me? nothing can affect the miserable. But I will endeavour to avail myself of the present moment; the air has revived me, the fever which consumes me, rages less violent; I will try if I can detail to you what appears to me a chaos of horror.

That passion, that unfortunate but violent passion, which I so long cherished for the most ungrateful of mankind, you well know. But still veiling it for ever under a carelessness of manner, bordering (I will acknowledge) on levity, I hoped to hide it from every eye but his. I did not desire that even himself should penetrate to the bottom of my soul; yet I know how quick-sighted is the vanity of man, and I believed he could not be ignorant of my sentiments towards him. Let me hasten through the degrading, hateful history, of my shame and disgrace.

Some few evenings previous to his departure, we met at a party; his carriage not arriving at the precise time he had ordered it, I, who was quitting the assembly, offered him, with secret joy, a seat in mine; happy (fool!) in any opportunity of enjoying his company. He condescended to accept my offer, (surely never had he appeared so charming in my infatuated eyes as on that evening) perhaps because it seemed to me he had paid me particular attention. True, indeed, I endeavoured to attach him as much as possible to myself, exclusively; for, comparing him with the crowd of ideots round, he shone like the god of day amid artificial lights. I could look at—I could speak to, none but him; nor could I endure to hear him compliment another female. I saw, or fancied that I saw, his eloquent orbs sparkle with pleasure at the marked preference I gave him over his humble contemporaries; the rich glow in his cheeks became more animated; I intoxicated myself with looking at him, but I was doomed to be rudely awakened, and toppled headlong from my visionary height.

On our way home, Wiemar essayed, with his usual taste and elegance, to converse on indifferent subjects; I answered him vaguely, abstractedly; for, strange to say, my mind was too full of the speaker to listen to what he was saying. I was wrapped up in the idea of him; perhaps, too, I was a little mortified that his discourse never once turned on love.— A length we reached my home, and Wiemar having conducted me up stairs, prepared (provoking creature) to take his leave; I begged him to be seated a moment; he remarked (I thought, with some slight embarrassment) the lateness of the hour.

" What is the calculation of time," said I, smiling, " in the enjoyment of pleasure, and that your society is a pleasure to me, I shall not affect to deny."

He bowed with that fascinating grace which is so peculiarly his own, and placed himself at the farther end of the sopha on which I had seated myself.

His frigid reserve and tantalizing politeness made me mad, but an irresistible fatality urged me on. I looked at him a moment in silence; how handsome he appeared! the distance of his manner could not alter him.

A single lamp, in an alabaster vase, cast a dim mysterious light through the apartment, and diffused over his majestic form a charm almost supernatural. His cheek, which at the assembly had been highly flushed, now, from the effect of the light or some other cause, appeared pale, while his dark eyes, severe even in their brightness, sparkled like two meteors through the glimmering shade in which he sat. As I continued to gaze on him, such powerful love rushed over my soul as completely overcame me; yes, I felt as though my fate depended on the fiat of that man!— I was no longer any thing of myself, my brain grew bewildered, and I placed my hand before my eyes to shut out his image, and, if possible, collect my ideas.

Wiemar observed my emotion; it was, no doubt, evident enough; I felt the blood rush to my cheeks and retreat again to my heart; my varying looks alarmed him; he flew towards me with that anxious benevolence which I always imagined made a part of his character; he tenderly leaned over me, took my hand

and held it; I endeavoured to raise my head; it drooped on his breast.

" "Lady Zulmer," he exclaimed, " speak, are you not well?—tell me what assistance can I render you?"

I could not answer.

" Appollonia! dear Lady Appollonia! I beseech you tell me but how you feel;" he anxiously reiterated, still bending over me.

His attitude, his soft, soothing voice, but above all, the epithet *dear*, which he had addressed to me, transported me beyond myself; ah! why should men occasion such emotion where they do not love? I raised my eyes to his face, and deeply sighing, I reclined my burning forehead on the hand which held mine.

"Wiemar," I faltered out, while I felt my cheeks glow with fire, "I feel—I feel that I love you—more than I can describe—that on you—on *you* depends my fate.

Had a thunderbolt fallen at the feet of the being before whom I thus, like a wretch, poured out the overflowing of my soul, he could not have appeared more aghast, more confounded! Had he felt a scorpion darting its sting into his breast, he could not more violently have started and recoiled! Had hell gaped beneath him, he could not have looked more enhorrored! Snatching his hand from the convulsed grasp of mine, he retreated backwards, unable to utter a sentence.

"You disdain me, then," said I, nered with the boldness of despair; "You despise me!"

" Certainly not," replied he with quickness, " certainly not—but—but—"

" But you do not," cried I; " you *never* can love me—is it not so ?"

" I—I really—pardon me—I had no idea that—I—"

Oh! my dear preceptress, pardon *me* the further delineation of this cruel scene. Suffice it, that urged on by unconquerable feelings, I goaded him to a firm unequivocal rejection of me. I goaded him, impelled by frenzy and despair, to acknowledge he never *had* loved me, and never *could;* that his attentions to me were purely those which he must ever pay to beauty and to talent; that I had an undoubted claim to them ; that he had never sought, or wished to excite an interest in my heart, and that he had ever conceived it as perfectly unattached as his own.

Perhaps, knowing my disposition, you may imagine that this avowal rendered me outrageous; that my rage and mortification transported me even beyond what my love had done. You tremble, no doubt, at the thought of the conflicting passions which you conceive shook my soul and agitated my frame. But the triumph was denied him, who had already triumphed too much, of beholding the despair and anguish of a woman scorned! the feelings I had, I restrained, and affected others that were foreign to my soul. A few moments, during which I was silent, sufficed me to collect my ideas and to decide my conduct; I saw the abyss to which I had degraded myself, and the sensation of shame I experienced, gave birth in my bosom to a *hatred which will never die.* I became deeply and eternally embittered against the man, who had *dared* to render me contemptible in my own eyes. I felt that nothing but his

destruction could wash out his offence, and
I determined on it; in my inmost heart
I secretly pledged myself to atchieve it or
to perish: the vow registered on that
faithful tablet *will in time be fulfilled.*

But it was necessary to raise myself in
the estimation of him who was prepared
to despise me, to inspire him with a new
and definable sensation for me, and since
it was impossible to make him love, make
him at least respect me, and desire to become my friend. To this end no great
artifice was requisite. Some slight management, and playing upon the susceptible feelings I knew him to possess, secured my point. The heart which had
been shut against me when *love* had been
the theme, expanded at the name of *friendship;* its emotions were nearly as powerful as love could have rendered them, nay
more powerful than the love of half the
cold-blooded mortals in the universe. He

seemed solicitous, under the name of friendship, to make me every reparation, to heal the wound he had given (as if that were possible) and under that misleading impulse he would have gone the greatest lengths. For my forbearance, he owes me eternal gratitude, for I had him completely in my power, and might have taken what advantage I thought proper of the warmth of his feelings.

I believe there are few moments more dangerous to man, or to woman either, than those when pity dissolves the heart; love may then easily enter, and would scarcely be detected or repulsed. But no, I scorned to owe my victory to an involuntary sensation. Appollonia take advantage of a weak moment!—besides, far dearer to me than the gratification of my love, was now become the gratification of my vengeance; it seemed more allied to my heart, more identified with my feelings, as it were.   I would not have resigned it, nor would I now, for all that ever Wiemar could give.

I suffered him to escape then in apparent security, but only to have him the more certain victim hereafter. I have set my mark on him; he is destined for the sacrifice, but till the hour arrives let him frolic and be gay, and wander where he will. This is all my consolation.

I now hasten to dismiss the theme, to tell you, that ere we parted, I bound the susceptible youth to me, by ties stronger than any he had yet experienced for me. I clearly perceive he never *could* have loved me; judging from his softness, his attentions, his looks, ever fraught with fire and animation, I conceived I had really inspired him with a passion ardent as that he had excited in me.   The event has proved my error, and, in so doing, developed his character to me, of which I had formed an estimate so wide of the reality. Be that as it may, I have known how to treat that character, to take due advantage of an over-teeming sensibility, and most unguarded frankness. I have brought myself off with all the honours of war, and my defeat even bears the splendid character of victory. I lost an imaginary lover, but gained a real friend.

Oh! men; ye lordly despots, what mere machines are you in the hands of those ye affect to govern; on what do ye ground your pretensions! for are ye not in reality *our* tools?

He left me, conceiving me to be an angel of goodness; a creature of superior elevated mind; arraigning himself bitterly for the pain he had inflicted on me, and for his stubborn insensibility in having

been unable to love me, as my fine qualities and virtues merited.

Thanks to your lessons of experience,
my dear gouvern'ante ; I have clearly proved in my commerce with the world, that
there is a certain infallible mode of treating every character under the sun, however difficult it may be. I believe I could
now find my way through the most intri-
çate windings of human nature : no
heart, though habergeoned by a triple
coat of steel could be guarded against
me. So should it be—*man* must believe
himself invested with sovereign power,
woman only should possess it.

Communicating with you has assuaged
my lacerated feelings ; I began my letter
in a state of madness—I wish I could
conclude it rationally and soberly. The indifference of Wiemar ought not to change
me, indeed, for it has not robbed me of

any thing, or made me worse than I was;
do I not yet see the gay world before me,
and behold myself still with youth, and
health, and beauty to enjoy it. You
will not think this last an extraordinary
observation, for surely beauty is a great
requisite to woman in the enjoyment of
life. Oh! of how many delightful moments—of what homage, of what power,
and pleasure, are those unfortunates de-
prived, who are slighted by nature! I,
then, possess every advantage for enjoyment; I will not then despair or grieve,
but neither will I, in the plenitude of exultation, forget, that *one* exists in the universe who has dared to disdain me.

Ah! do you know I lost a considerable
sum last night, my dear gouvernante; if I
go on thus I shall speedily be ruined;
you have often cautioned me against this
destructive vice, in vain. During the life-
time of Count Zulmer, I had no other re-

source from the ennui of his society;
since I have been my own mistress, I am
sorry to say it has gained upon me; but
I have always endeavoured to persuade myself that in time I might make some use
of it as a talent: hitherto, however, I
have been unfortunate, for certainly it has
not *increased* my resources. Yet,—Oh!
why do I now plunge with such avidity
into the madness of high play?—Why?
but to save me from greater madness. If,
before it was to rescue me from melancholy, it is now to preserve me from distraction!——Yes, yes! I confess what it
were in vain to deny; it is—to drive
Wiemar, the traitor and fugitive, from
my thoughts. I must rouse myself, or
sink into despair: I court ruin rather
than *think*—weakly think. Is it not better
to contemplate beggary, than ponder
over the insult I have received? I endeavour to lose the memory of my abase-
ment by any means, but all are equally

vain; I still behold myself a wretch, bearing about me the marks of indelible disgrace, and imagine every one reads in my countenance the shame I have undergone.

Would you believe that, in addition to all the misery I have suffered, I have been assailed by those minor torments to which all great characters must, more or less, be subject?—I mean the tools—the instruments, by which we effect our pleasure.

The base Mondovi, and the wretched creature of his will, Catherine Glatz, would leave me no interval of repose.—I am almost tempted to defy them—but prudence, to which the most enterprising genius must sometimes bow, I believe says no Adieu, dearest friend! I have become exhausted with the violence of my emotions, and languid for want of rest; the

hour is late ; I will try and court sleep—
a blessing I have not for long enjoyed.

LETTER V.

MADAME DE HAUTVILLE TO THE COUN-
TESS APPOLLONIA ZULMER.

Strasburgh.

WELL, my dear child, I acknowledge
the commencement of your letter terrified
me to that degree, I thought I should
never have courage to get to the end of it.
I endeavoured to persevere, however, and
found you, towards the close, recovering
your senses, though you soon lost them a-
gain. I could never have believed, after the
lessons of philosophy I was at such pains
to inculcate in you, that either you would
have permitted yourself to fall a prey to

love, or have experienced the smallest anxiety at the coldness of another.

Did I not always describe love to you as the most insane, and at the same time the most dangerous of all passions for a woman? Did I not always tell you, that love was the destruction of woman's power and glory?—witness the fools it makes of men. Well, a woman in love is always worse; because, with stronger feelings, her reason is weaker—her power of resistance less. While woman preserves her heart secure, her empire is boundless; she may do what she will, and will what she please; but the moment her heart becomes touched, she is as a dethroned king, and those who were her vassals, become masters. Men have too many triumphs—it is a subject of congratulation to me, that I was never guilty of the folly of adding to them, and I had even ventured to flatter myself, that I had placed one more of my sex on the same eminence. As I had no fortune, I very early discovered that it would be the height of absurdity for me to fall in love; I therefore prudently determined against it, and what is more, I kept my resolution.

There was a young man, a farmer, in the village where I lived, conceived, as he said, a great affection for me, but he was no richer than myself, and I wondered at his folly. Love and a cottage were not analogous to my ideas, I was not formed for the calm, domestic life; I did all I could think of to throw myself forward, but for long in vain.

At last, when I began to despair, and accuse nature for having given me such soaring ideas in so circumscribed a sphere, a rich merchant came to settle in our village for the benefit of his health.

This revived my sinking hopes; I laboured hard that he should become acuainted with me, which in a little time ae did. I saw that a good nurse would be of more advantage to him than fine air, and I ventured, accidentally as it were, to insinuate as much. The idea ravished him, and, to my inexpressible joy, he soon made me an offer of his hand, gallantly telling me, that his heart had been mine from the first moment he had beheld me. I was indifferent as to the sincerity or falsehood of that part of his declaration; but, with an eagerness and delight, it cost me more pain than ever I felt in my life to disguise; 1 accepted his offer, and we were united.

That great point arranged so perfectly to my satisfaction, I soon persuaded my spouse, that change of air, and enlivening his spirits by amusement, would be the most effectual way of restoring him to

perfect health. He took my advice, and
a week after my nuptials, the little white
house, where my kind husband, while a
single man, had peacefully resided, was
forsaken for ever, and a fine lodging in
Paris, (for it was the *air of Paris* I fixed
on to complete his recovery) in one of
the first hotels received us instead ;—
change in my estimation how superior !

Alas ! at best, we are but short-sighted
mortals ; as soon as we were established in
Paris, in a style befitting the great fortune
of my husband, I launched, as you may
readily suppose, into every extravagance
of luxury, dress, equipage ; every amusement that money could procure I eagerly
essayed.

My tender husband remonstrated—it
was in vain ; I hired him an excellent
nurse, which he had never once thought
of doing for himself, and had then per-

fect leisure to dedicate to the invention of new pleasures.

At length my husband, finding that, according to this plan of things, his enormous riches would speedily be diminished, readily embraced a proposal which was made him of embarking in a scheme, which was ridiculously vaunted as capable of producing treble interest for money, without the smallest comparative risk. He now conceived that he had hit upon an excellent expedient for securing a part of his property from my rapacious craving, and he embarked nearly two-thirds of what he possessed in this mad scheme, congratulating himself all the time on his Machiavelian arrangement. He was justly punished, however, for his folly and meanness, at which I should have rejoiced, but that I was myself involved, for the scheme ended in a bubble, and my wise husband became a beggar. This broke his heart, and I was undone.

I looked round me, and discovered that after a few years spent in extravagant pleasure and idle folly, I now stood in the world, in regard to fortune, as near as possible upon an equality with the point from which I had started, with this small and somewhat inconvenient shadow of difference, however, that I was a few years older. I was just as a traveller, who, determining on a race to get the sooner to the end of his journey, misses through eager impatience, his way, and after much labour and fatigue, brings himself, by a circuitous rout, to the same spot he sat out from. This being the case, like a sea-beaten mariner driven ashore—(another simile for you) I made a collection of the wrecks, and applied to the compass of my wits for what course next to steer.

A second husband to my taste I durst not hope for—what must be done? In poverty the mind is paralysed, there is scarcely a possibility of exertion, and the fire of genius is counteracted by its freezing influence. I therefore was proposing to resign myself to my fate, when a female friend, with whom in my gay hours I had been in the habits of associating, taking pity on my forlorn state, made me the offer (how degrading should I once have thought it) of becoming the gouvernante her children.

With joy did I accept of this situation; for I flattered myself I should again behold something of life, and my heart was not yet dead to its pleasures. In a short time I figured in this new character which fortune had thought proper to cast for me; I succeeded to admiration, and gave the highest satisfaction to my employer, because, my means of livelihood depending so entirely upon my means of pleasing, I exerted myself solely to that point, and found no difficulty in it, for nature had gifted me with a vast flexibility of disposition, and at the same time forborne to trouble me with too much sensibility I easily reconciled myself to my situation, and made use of my great sheet anchor in my progress through the world, *flattery;* for flattery, my dear Appollonia, is pleasing to the very wisest of us, and those who are *not* wise, love us the better for it. One always finds the advantage of putting people in good humour with themselves; and what does it cost us? *Self* is the idol of every one, though few will acknowledge the stubborn fact, but self is nevertheless the centre, round which the passions move.

After I had been some time in the department last mentioned, you were introduced to the family. You were a poor

little orphan, left an unwelcome legacy
to them, by your parents, who were dis-
tantly related to them, and who died in
such poverty as to be incapable of leaving
you any claim to consideration—I mean
any fortune. You made your appearance, of course, under most unfavourable
auspices. To do justice, however, to
those among whom you were thrown,
they treated you kindly enough at first,
but you soon grew extraordinarily handsome, and as they had daughters of their
own, their kindness changed to coldness.

Believe me, or not, my dear Appollonia,
after my frank avowals to you of the
faults of my character, but I loved you
the moment I saw your little unfriended
face; I conceived the determination of doing all for you that laid in my power,
and I soon perceived you would repay me
most amply for my attention. You were

a most ductile child to me, and as you were poor as I had been, and still was, I thought it would be for your advantage to fashion you on my own principles, and give you besides the benefit of my experience.

How admirably I succeeded with you ! Do you not well remember when first the old Count Zulmer appeared ? how eagerly every one endeavoured to secure him; but your superior beauty, aided by my counsels, and the conduct I prescribed for your adoption, bore him off triumphantly. You became the Countess Zulmer ! You ! the poor little despised orphan ! the fortuneless, humble dependant ! Yes, you became the Countess Zulmer, and looked down in your turn on those who had slighted you !

Well my dear pupil, did you compensate my care and anxiety for you; I always fancied you were destined to become at one time or another of eminent service to me; the event has not deceived me. The moment you were married, you took me to your home, and your further affection in securing me a portion for my future comfort, now smooths the decline of my life, and enables me to pass it in tranquillity. Yes, my dear, grateful child, I say tranquillity, for that is now my only wish; it suits best with my increasing years. Bustle, animation, and gaiety are for youth; and when we are capable of enjoying pleasure; but to me, quiet and ease are now the greatest enjoyments.

It is to you, my dearest Appollonia, that I owe the possession of them. Amply did you reward my exertions to render you independent, by rendering *me* so. You, too, feel the happiness of being your own mistress. Contrast your situation with

that which you endured in the family
of your proud envious relations! Can
you ever sufficiently rejoice at your eman-
cipation from such illiberal tyranny?

But you did not at the time properly
appreciate the husband I selected for
you; yet had I chosen you a young man,
what might now have been your fate!—
probably that of a wretched slave, you
might only have exchanged your bondage,
for *young men* are insufferably despotic,
and often embitter to the last moment
of her existence the fate of the woman
who is unfortunate enough to become
united to them. But the poor Count
Zulmer! no sooner had he obtained the
unspeakable felicity which he sighed for,
the possession of your hand, than in gratitude for the favour he hastened to leave
you to the exclusive enjoyment of all the
riches he possessed. He could do no less,

certainly, for to have remained too long, would have counteracted the benefit he conferred by marrying you.

Well! my dear child, I hope I have talked, or rather written you into better spirits, and that you will never more begin a letter to me in such a doleful strain as your last—no, never let me receive one like it—it would unnerve me for a week.

But I am most truly concerned to find, that you have not yet divested yourself of that most unfortunate propensity, I mean gaming. Surely your mind is strong enough to abandon, if you resolved on it, even *settled* habits, much less acquired ones. Think how destructive a one is this. I confess myself astonished a person of your philosophic turn, can be for an instant attached to so ruinous a frivolity, in my opinion too, one so wholly unattractive. Would you ever, my dear

child, you who have experienced the horrors of dependance wish again to re-
duce yourself to poverty ? If you do
not—then leave high play to fools,—to
those vacant minds who have nothing else
to occupy or interest them, and who, re-
quiring some petty exercise to keep their
drowsy faculties from stagnating, throw
bits of painted paper at one another,
that they may continue feebly to vacil-
late : there is no excuse for *you*—reflect
often on your nearly concluding lines—
they were rational and just. Yes, my
dear Apollonia you have still the gay
world before you, and youth, and health,
and beauty, to enjoy it. Do not despond,
as if you were as old, and as ugly as I am.
For my part I have no longer a taste for
the world, I could not derive the least
enjoyment from mingling in the crowd,
neither, probably, will you at my age.
But at present—*love no one*, range the
narrow circle of pleasure, waste no more

precious moments in grieving for a worthless man, while there are hundreds who would be too happy in your smiles. Despise him, I advise, and dismiss him from your thoughts, and let the temporary pain you have suffered, operate as a suficient warning to you, however you admit again a *preference* to your bosom, or fix for a single instant your hopes of happiness on the *gratitude* of man.

I had almost forgotten your observations with respect to that wretch Mondovi—no, I would not have you defy him; since unfortunately you have placed yourself in his power, you must buy his discretion at a high price; patience where there is no remedy Besides, by keeping him your slave, which gold will do, he may probably still be useful to you, whereas, by irritating him, you can gain nothing and may do yourself much mischief. When once a villain has been of service, there is no plan but ever after to retain him, by the only bond he will acknowledge—interest. Adieu, my dear child, write me speedily that you are perfectly recovered from the effects of your late delirium.

LETTER VI.

PIETRO MONDOVI TO CATHERINE GLATZ.

I TELL thee thou art a fool, and wilt never be otherwise—thou knowest not how to deal with our slippery Countess. Thou askest for thine own as if it were matter of favour. Is she not indebted then to us? Have we done her no service? Is she not in our power? Could we not unmask and make her tremble. Thou knowest not how to avail thyself of our

advantages. What is her fancied elevation? what is her rank in society? Could
we not speedily topple her from her
height by shewing her such as she is? I
tell thee again, thou art a fool, and knowest not how to deal with her, and thy
folly will blast all our prospects, and all
the hopes thou cherishest, for be assured
I will never unite myself to thee and beggary. Thy good name, therefore, may remain for ever unretrieved by me. If yielding to what I prescribed to thee thou hadst
taught our Countess to know I would neither be sported with nor cajoled, it would
have been better for thee.

To make amends for thy ill-timed cour-
tesy, tell her I charge thee without further delay, that the sum I have demanded I *must* have, and that, ere three days
more elapse. What! shall I have nothing
to compensate me, for the twinges I sometimes feel for having executed her com-

mands ? nothing to console me under the heavy penance that the holy father Anselmo would inflict on me if he knew of half that I have done?　Can the mischief I have caused my poor soul in the hopes of earthly gain be ever repaid? and to stand the damage for nothing, I say, would not that be a sorry piece of business?　I am determined, therefore, as what is done is not to be undone, to make the most of my wickedness—1 am sorry that word has slipped out, but let it go. Since I cannot retrieve the past, I must allow no thought to have sway, but how best I can profit by it.　I write in a dull strain methinks, but I am always out of spirits when I am poor.　The sight of the money will set all to rights. I expect it impatiently—farewel—be wise if thou canst, and above all be prompt.

LETTER VII.

CATHERINE GLATZ TO THE COUNTESS ZULMER.

Efferden.

THIS is to inform your ladyship that I received, the other day, a visit from Pietro Mondovi. He said he had business through this town, and that he took my cottage in his way, but I humbly beg to observe to your ladyship, that I believe the real purport of his visit was to tell me what he hoped I should repeat to you.

Pietro Mondovi, your ladyship well knows, was always one that kept a steady eye to his own interest, and with all due deference I wonder you would ever employ him in your service. He said he had a hard matter to live, owing to people who promised highly and performed slenderly. When people were served, he remarked, and had got all smooth before them, they were apt to be forgetful. He added that, for his part, he could do no longer without money, and he must have some by one means or other. He then concluded by abruptly asking me when I had heard from your ladyship.

I told him I had heard lately and was going to write to you. " Well! well,' answered he roughly, " when you do, tell her I called on you. You understand me," with a significant look.

I coolly replied that I should inform your ladyship, which accordingly I have thought it my duty to do, hoping you will not be offended.

As for myself, I long for nothing so

much as for an opportunity of rendering your ladyship some further services, you having been pleased so bountifully to acknowledge what little I have ever had it in my power to perform for you; no more, indeed, than my duty, since inferiors should ever bow to the commands of their superiors, when they are generous.

I will not any longer take up your ladyship's time at present, only begging you to believe I am ever the humble servant of your pleasure.

I forgot to tell your ladyship Pietro mentioned something about being in immediate want of three hundred crowns.

LETTER VIII.

THE COUNTESS ZULMER TO PIETRO MONDOVI.

Vienna.

PIETRO MONDOVI,

I AM sorry to hear from Catherine Glatz that you are distressed for money. Had I known you were so hard driven I should cheerfully have inconvenienced my-self to have assisted you; though to be plain with thee, I have had a run of ill-luck for these some weeks past; fortune appears to have turned her back on me, and I am at this moment poorer compa-ratively than thou canst be. It will not be long so, I trust, but at all events I have contrived to send thee rather better than the half of what thou requirest, with which I hope thou wilt be content for a while, until I can further acknowledge thy good services.

But, I must tell thee, Pietro, I am somewhat displeased with thee for murmuring and complainin to Catherine— t sets a bad precedent; I trust thou wilt have more consideration for the future. Believe me, sincerely, thine.

LETTER IX.

PIETRO MONDOVI TO THE COUNTESS ZULMER.

I RETURN your ladyship my humble thanks, for your ladyship's kind notice of my request, and entreat your pardon for having offended you by my complaints. My extreme poverty, indeed, is my sole excuse; I endeavoured, through the medium of Catherine, to refresh your memory with my humble claims on your bounty. That your ladyship has so promptly acknowledged them, fills me with gratitude;—but Catherine Glatz was a fool, (and your ladyship knows she was never very wise) to give you to understand that I insinuated aught against your ladyship. I only spoke of my wants, and said I wished you could think of them; indeed, the money which your ladyship has sent me, will go to the payment of a heavy debt I have unavoidably contracted, but if the rich often contract debts, which they cannot pay, there may be some excuse for the poor.

LETTER X.

BARON ROZENDORF TO COUNT DARLO-WITZ.

Vienna.

No, my dear Darlowitz, no; it is in vain; I have passed the gay meridian of youth, and my habits are settled. After this declaration, it is but a poor compliment to you, to say that if any thing could induce me to alter my ideas, it would be your glowing description of the joys of wedded life.*

It is true that the strict and ardent friendship which we formed when

---

* The letter to which this is an answer does not appear.

boys together at the university of Leipzic,
implied a certain congeniality of idea,
that to a casual observer of the human
mind, would have made it appear probable, our course and pursuits through life
would be ultimately much influenced by
one another.

But, in fact, though our souls were congenial, our dispositions and pursuits were
even then different—you were all spirit,
ardour, and enthusiasm, nothing could
restrain your impetuosity. The advice of
friends you loved could not check you in
a favourite vagary; and, often hurried
away by the infatuation of the moment,
the vivacity of your passions overcame
your better reason. But your errors, my
dear Darlowitz, served only as foils to
your virtues; your head wandered, but
your heart was never in the wrong; and,
if I may be allowed a solecism, you would
have been less amiable without them.

Our Wiemar was an enthusiast too, but of a different description. He was a refined enthusiast—delicate, sentimental, and susceptible on certain points, to a degree sufficient to become the cause of infinite misery to him, should ever his feelings be too powerfully awakened. There was a tincture of melancholy in his disposition that unfitted him to be the partner of your wild wanderings; but that melancholy was of a sublime character, elevating his soul, yet attempering it to the softest emotions of friendship; he loved us both with an entireness and confidence of affection, that powerfully interested, and drew our hearts towards him.

With respect to myself, if I may be allowed to form a judgment, it appears to me, that though I possessed neither the ardent temperament of the one, nor the refined susceptibility of the other, yet I ɩesembled both in spirit—in the character of the soul; and, as in chemistry, ingredients the most opposite to each other, shall yet possess in their elements certain principles of assimilation, causing them readily to combine, so those points of attraction which existed in our apparently dissimilar characters, caused us to harmonize in the most perfect union.

In early youth, though the character is not formed, it bears strong outlines of what it will become, as a sketch by the hand of a master will give an idea of the picture yet to be filled up. It does not seem to me, that either of us have deviated widely from what we then appeared; you, perhaps, are somewhat sobered; youth has ebullitions which naturally subside as we approach manhood, and the judgment, matures. You are not now so eager, so wild, in the pursuit of any object that strikes your fancy : you have learnt better

to appreciate in what true happiness consists, and experience has evinced to you,
that it is not in the desultory and profitless
research after eternal novelty. The eye,
from viewing a variety of glowing co·
lours, becomes fatigued, and loves to rest
on the " soft green" of nature : so it is
with the mind; a succession of pleasure
palls and wearies, and the heart wishes for
repose. This is best to be found in the
bosom of domestic life, surrounded by the
tender and dear relations that accompany
it, and where the emotions that are excited,
distract not by their violence, but tend to
harmonize the soul, and fill it with a sense
of happiness: this brings me back to the
point from which I set out. You naturally ask me, why with this sensibility to,
and disposition for, domestic enjoyment,
do I persist in remaining isolated in the
midst of a crowd?

This very sensibility is the cause, my

dear Darlowitz. I am a timid, apprehensive creature, and dread disappointment.
If, with my (perhaps romantic) ideas of
domestic felicity, I should wed in the
hope of realizing them—If I should raise
my expectations too high, and then—*if*—
oh! this terrible little word, how much
does it involve.—There is a possibility, at
all events, of my finding, that my brilliant
dream would not stand the test of waking
proof; my fairy fabric might not be ten-
able for real life. I should not have fortitude to endure, what, at least, I may have
firmness to avoid the chance of encountering. Do not endeavour to impair that
firmness; for, should I ever yield to your
solicitations, and seriously think of iden-
tifying my destiny with that of a wife,
perhaps you would have to regret the influence you had exerted over your friend.

I adore the lovely sex; I adore them,
too much to marry. I consider them, as I

do the religion of Mahomet, which I admire for its wildness, beauty, and seduction, while I see its errors, extravagance,
and inconsistency ; I would not ground
my hopes of happiness on the fallacious-
ness of the one, or the other. The character of women has engaged much of my
observation. Few are the exceptions to
be made, when I must say that generally
speaking, they are not calculated to be
sources of lasting happiness to man.
There is a weakness, a frivolity about
them, resulting at once from their nature
and education. They want character,
stamina. They are the fragile barks of
pleasure, sailing swiftly and gaily up the
stream of life; not the firm majestic vessel, formed to breast the storm, or to
which securely one may trust. No, woman! lovely, amiable, enchanting woman! Ye are the gentle light of our
souls! ye are as the promethean fire, by
which we are animated, but we should

not dwell too near you, lest we be consumed by your power.

Few men, my Darlowitz, can expect or hope to meet with a treasure such as you possess. Amelia is the perfection of womankind; she has, concentrated in herself every rare quality, every admirable endowment, which is dispersed among the sex at large, and to them she has superadded a strength, and sublimity of character, entirely her own, such as I solemnly affirm never to have beheld the least particle of in any other female. Oh! cherish her, my friend! cherish her with admiring awe, in the inmost core of your heart, for such a creature is alone sufficient to redeem half the sex from their insignificance. As you are sensible of your supreme felicity, so may you long continue to enjoy it, and may you experience a second era of bliss in your children.

LETTER XI.

COUNT DARLOWITZ TO BARON ROZEN-DORF.

Lintz.

MY dear Rozendorf, were you always such a cynic with regard to women? I never heard you express your sentiments of them with so much severity. But I ought not to be surprised, for till I became a husband, I never considered them capable or worthy of inspiring a lasting attachment.

Oh! how am I now changed, it is in married life only that the virtues of women are developed; it is in married life only that we learn how to value them. Upon retracing my past existence, and comparing it with my present, what a blank does it appear to me! What an uninteresting idle period! Now, what solid happiness do I not experience! What tender delicious ties wind round my heart; what various sources of exquisite and rational delight has the possession of my Amelia opened to me; her whom so justly, so truly you characterise as the superior of women.

Oh! my dear Rozendorf, it *is* when overflowing with the delicious consciousness of the happiness I enjoy, when a thousand tender sensations, resulting from my situation, crowd on my heart, that I so press you to marry: but I should remember, indeed, that there is no second Amelia, or you would not hesitate.—Highly as you appreciate her, you know not the thousandth part of her excellencies in each department of her life, as a wife, a mother, a friend.—In her there is nothing frivolous or vain; she is, to

use your own metaphor, "the firm majestic vessel that could breast the storm."
Formed on such a model, it is impossible
for her children not to be virtuous. Could
you witness her exemplary conduct, my
Rozendorf, how she devotes herself to
them and to me! How active she is in
every duty of domestic life; yet, how
elegant, how chearful, how much at her
ease, in her manners and conversation—
for ever employed, yet for ever unembarrassed; serious, dignified, yet unaffected; learned, yet diffident; keenly perceiving error, yet never severe; penetrating, yet making no parade of her
discernment. Conscious of the value she
is of, in the midst of her family, yet not
appearing to be so; knowing, as she
must, that she is faultless, yet meek and
unassuming as an angel.

The early part of the morning she de-
dicates to study, I should say rather to

the refreshment of her mind, for she is well
versed in almost every species of useful and
refined literature. The ancient classic and
the best modern authors, are familiar to
her; yet, that she is no pedant, Rozendorf,
thou well knowest---a character so detestable in a female. Then, like the bee,
laden with sweets, she carries all the honey to her hive, that is to say, to the
room where her children are assembled,
already expecting her, her girls and her
two youngest boys. There she passes
two hours in instructing them; she afterwards accompanies the dear creatures
in a ramble if the weather any way
permit: I am frequently of the party,
or I soon follow, or meet them, but
we always return together. Some time
is then dedicated to the necessary business, not of intellectual, but physical refreshment; and oh! can you conceive a
more interesting group? can you imagine
a more happy situation for a man, than

to sit at his table,—his wife, like the mother of the graces, smiling beside him;
and his children, with animated faces, in
which young rising genius, and happiness
and innocent affection, are pourtrayed,
ranged around! No, it is the heaven of
earth! there is no bliss beyond it.

The evening is devoted at once to pleasure
and improvement in the fine arts. Amelia
has a melodious voice; the tones of her
eldest, Frederick, have something sublime
in them; she sings, and plays the harp;
I take my violin, one of my boys a flute;
all subscribe either their voice or their
music, we have an exquisite, and as we conceive, a masterly concert. Sometimes
we prefer a dance; or if the night be fine
or tempting, we go into the garden. I
have an excellent telescope, and my children acquire something of astromony; or
we make experiments, or studying by
moonlight the various effects of light and
shade, we turn it to account in painting

transparencies in an unique style, sketching
with terrific sublimity, dark-browed mountains, ruins, and distant gleaming ghosts.

Thus, my friend, in speaking of Amelia, have I been led to give you some picture of my domestic felicity; that felicity,
which as she intrinsically constitutes,
must always accompany her idea. Perhaps, however, it may answer a better
purpose than any representation or en-
treaty I could make use of, to induce
you to adventure among us; you might
participate in our happiness at least, without any risk, if you are determined
against hazarding your own, in the possible chance of connubial disappointment. But on this point I will urge nothing, as no man is justified in interrupt-
ing the system of another, congenial to his
ideas, unless he can promise him superior happiness in the event of his aban-
doning it.

Have you heard from Wiemar since he has quitted Vienna? I have had from him but one solitary letter; I begin to fear he has forgotten us amid the enlightened rustics of Switzerland, whom he praises so highly.

LETTER XII.

COUNT WIEMAR TO BARON ROZENDORF.

Zurich.

ROZENDORF! my soul has caught a glimpse of a creature who appears the prototype, the original of the image pourtrayed by my youthful imagination, and acknowledged still by my maturer reason. Not an Appollonia—no; this glimpse which I have caught, has convinced me how erroneously I should have acted, if, yielding to a romantic punctilio of false honour, I had resigned my fate into the hands of that female who was never destined for me by nature, and for whom I experienced in my breast no single sentiment that gave intimation of our souls being congenial. Mine was never attracted towards her; there were no principles of amalgamation in our elements; composed of qualities the most opposite to each other, no art, no endeavours, could have made us blend. What is irreconcilable by nature can never be reconcilable to right: had I become the husband of Appollonia, I should have outraged her immutable laws, which forbid disunion, which are maintained by harmony, and I should have been punished for my folly with consequent misery. But oh! the fair being, who has passed like some bright vision before me—think me a wild enthusiast if you will—she, or none, must be mine.

And was it decreed then, that flying from one I could not love to bury myself in these solitudes, faithful to the voice of nature in my heart, refusing to outrage her, I should be thus supremely reward-ed? Was it decreed, that in these pro-found retreats alone, I must seek for, and behold the creature who could make me happy?

But, whither am I wandering? how know I yet if such bliss may be mine? What! have I only *seen* her, scarcely heard her, and already do I feel these pow-erful emotions! Yes! 'tis even so; the instant I beheld her, she revived the pic-tured beauty in my fancy; it was her likeness which long had dwelt there, and I recognised instantly the model. Na-ture, I repeat, is ever true to herself; I should not have felt these powerful emo-tions on beholding one who was to be afterwards indifferent to me, or in whose fate mine should never bear a part; what she awakened was sympathy—she touched chords which vibrated to her; her beauty was less the cause of the emotion she inspired, than the previous state of my soul on which her presence acted. There must be times, my Rozendorf, I am assured of it, perhaps during sleep, when the soul, disembodied, takes an excursive flight, and almost glances into the future. Hence the images and associations which become formed in our mind, otherwise unaccountable; hence, too, the ideas and anticipations, which frequently influence us, we know not why, through life, remain often in defiance to the existing appearances of things, and hold despotic sway over our actions.

Have you never felt on any particular event occurring to you, as if it was not wholly unexpected, yet without any definable cause for anticipating it? Have you never been in scenes in which you appeared to yourself to have been before? Has no realization ever called to your mind thoughts, and pre-sentiments, which at the time were unheeded?—Perhaps not.—I know that you do not, like me, give the loose reins to imagination. I suffer it to take too wild flights, doubtless; but whatever I may believe of the soul sometimes diving into the events of futurity, I do not pretend, like the Pythagorean philosopher, to retain any recollection of having *lived before*.

> " E'en I, who these mysterious truths declare,——
> " Was *once* Euphortus in the Trojan war,
> " My name, and lineage, I *remember well*,
> " And how in fight by Sparta's king *I fell*;
> " In Argive, Juno's fane, I *late* beheld
> " My buckler hung on high, *and own'd my former shield*."
>
> OVID'S METAM. Book xv.

Yet I am a creature so sensitive, so alive to impression, that the passing gale, wafting to me the fragrance of some particular plant or flower, will revive in my mind, by indefinable association, entire scenes of my life, most pleasing to me.— A sudden recollection, apparently not occasioned by any external object or occurrence, will sometimes flash on memory incidents of my childhood, expressions and even thoughts attendant on that period—I am led progressively on to my present state, and then beyond it.

Often, when a boy, have I listened to the deafening roar of the cataract, and, in the pleasing distraction occasioned by its noise formed the wildest fancies. Often have I laid myself down by the babbling brook, and while the warm sun-beams played on my closed lids, lost in a sort of delicious trance, I have wandered amid the most brilliant scenes. Sometimes dissolved in tender pleasure by the blandness of the air, and the fragrance round me, I have imagined myself lying at the feet of some nymph-like beauty, or in soft inter-

course straying with her through delightful meads.

Always in my boyish dreams of love,
the same fair image was the goddess of my,
idolatry—the same sweet figure swam in
my sight.—Whether I reclined by day on
the brink of the rivulet, or roamed by
night along the side of the mountain, she
never varied ;—the lovely vision became
stamped on my heart, and bore a part in
my existence. I became enamoured with
the being of my creative fancy ; I looked
around among women for her likeness, but
in vain; yet I could not but persuade
myself that in some spot of the earth—in
some other clime, she might exist, and I
might one day meet with her—at least I
indulged the romantic hope. I did not delude myself, I have discovered her. Yes, at
length I have discovered her, and amid
plains as beautiful, and scenes as wildly
picturesque, as ever I imagined to roam

with her. The same sylphid form—the samé bewitching softness and grace—even the very drapery—all, all reminded me of the visionary maiden of my boyish enthusiasm !

Mere accident was the means of my beholding her ; by her own consent, I have seen her only once since. I am as yet unacquainted with her history, situation, or the particular circumstances which have placed her in this retired part of the globe.

All I have been enabled to learn, is, that her name is Julia de Montalban, that she resides with her mother in the small cottage which they purchased when first they came hither, and that they are supposed to be persons of rank, driven by misfortune into this seclusion ; that they have already resided here several years, and are highly respected by the few with whom they deign to associate.

If all this be correct, what happiness may not be mine!—what obstacles can intervene to banish for ever my springing hopes? If she be well born, and of rank, she is undoubtedly well educated; if her mother be worthy of such a daughter, she has instilled proper principles into her mind. She has even in these profound solitudes still rendered her capable of ornamenting the highest sphere.—Should all this then be as I conceive, her want of fortune will be a grand concomitant in my favour; for to be thrown upon the world in poverty, and possessed of such rare charms and perfections, with all that simplicity and ignorance of society, necessarily resulting from her seclusion, would it not be destruction? I could shield her from every ill: her mother would not, could not, hesitate to place her tender child in honourable happy safety—to assure her of protection after she shall be no more.

Ah! let me not go too far, so bright, so clear, the prospect appears before me, I almost fear to contemplate it, lest gazing too intensely, I should discern some speck in the horizon, some distant gathering cloud. I should not reason thus on possibilities, and fix my happiness on the chance of contingencies. Yet oh! how vain this reflection! I feel—yes Rozendorf, I feel that my happiness is inextricably involved with Julia! Julia! yes— that name was ever pleasing to me; was ever music in my ears, and always accompanied my idea of female loveliness; I gave it to the fair vision of my boyish homage, it vibrates now on my ear—on my heart, like the sweet rushing sound of an Æolian harp. I heard her mother call her by her name, how musical! how harmonious it sounded! and above all, how *familiar* to my soul.

"What is there in a name?" I hear

my wise Rozendorf exclaim. Nothing indeed, exclusively considered; it derives all its sweetness or interest from the object who bears it, and the name of a beautiful person is only charming to our ear, because it instantly recals the idea of beauty to the mind. It is the *association* which produces the impression. Were Julia called by any other name, I should equally love it, because it would equally revive in my mind the perfections of her to whom it belongs.

Perhaps it may be a misfortune to possess a disposition such as mine, for though keenly alive to pleasure, and, in the ardor of imagination, exalting it to rapture, still am I no less susceptible of pain or disappointment: the measure is equal, and if I *enjoy* more exquisitely than the common lot of mankind, I likewise *suffer* more severely.

You my friend, though possessed of an energetic soul, a generous susceptible mind, and a heart formed for the tenderest emotions of friendship, are yet never hurried away by impetuosity of feeling. All your sentiments are virtues, all your virtues inherent, they require no effort; it is more easy to you, because more congenial, to be excellent than to err; and I am persuaded you would do yourself a violence in committing the least of those follies which are so common in the world. But although you are as perfect as man can be, no one ever heard you speak harshly of the imperfections of others. Although you are not in the least romantic, no one ever found you cold or indifferent, and though violent passions could never exercise dominion over you, how deeply can you feel for, and compassionate those, over whom they do.

To your precepts, my Rozendorf, your

fine and rational counsels, infinitely am I
indebted : to your tenderness and lenity
for my failings, to your kind toleration of
my extravagancies. Oh ! my Rozendorf,
you are, and ever were to me, a truly in-
valuable friend. You shall ever be the
depository of all my secrets, my faithful
best adviser. Even my feelings shall be
laid open to you, your eye will benevo-
lently scan, and appreciate them, you will
never be severe or unjust in your stric-
tures; in you fearlessly may I confide,
and without hesitation lay open my
breast; you shall know all, the progress,
as you already know the beginning of my
love; I will impart to you all my movements, my wishes, even my sensations.
Farewel; this evening I hope again to
behold and to converse with her; yes, to
behold and to converse with Julia; with
her, long the idol of my imagination. Can
it be that in sober waking reason I shall
behold her? no longer an unsubstantial

airy nothing, but the beauteous realization of springing life and health !

———

LETTER XIII.

BARON ROZENDORF TO COUNT WIEMAR.

Vienna.

HOW sweet my Wiemar is the praise of friendship ! how pleasing, how gratifying your letter to my soul ; yes, you say truly, you need not fear to confide to your Rozendorf, the most secret movements of your breast. In every case shall I ardently study your happiness and your good ; and by appealing to me when you are yourself in doubt, you affix a responsibility on me to guide you with scrupulous care in the best path.

I must now assume the character of

censor, and tell you that you do indeed,
my dear friend, give the reins too unre-
servedly to that mighty queen of your
brain, imagination. You mount your
Pegasus and soaring to heights unknown,
such weak mortals as myself strain after
you in vain! Not that I would have thee
wholly repress thy springing ardour either,
or that sublime enthusiasm, which forms so
grand a feature in the beauty of thy character to sink, if it were possible, into tame
insensibility, or content thyself with cold-
blooded calculations. No—but I would
wish thee for thine own peace sake, to
confine thine ideas more within the verge
of the *probable*, than let them wander to
the utmost extent of the barely *possible*.

It sometimes happens in man's life,
certainly, that things the most unlooked
for and extraordinary, come to pass, but
that is no argument for the indulgence of
extravagant or chimerical anticipations.

The secret of the transmutation of metals may possibly be yet discoverable, but we must nevertheless account him a fool who should expend his life and substance in the search.

Forgive this reasoning, my Wiemar. It is possible you may have found the being who can give you happiness, but it is little short of madness to rest your sole expectations of it on the realization of those hopes you have permitted yourself to conceive. Such a creature as you have imagined, *may* exist indeed, may exist even in her you have seen ; you may have identified your visionary fair, but may not a thousand obstacles likewise intervene to prevent you from obtaining her ? Of all delusions, beware those of the imagination, the heart is readily seduced by them. The ardent mind, disgusted with the monotonous occurrences and realities of common life, seeks for pleasure in excursive

flights, amid the brighter realms of fancy.
Reason at first condemns, but impercepti-
bly yields to the enticement. The danger
then is obvious, man becomes the victim
of a visionary system. He has allowed
himself to pause enchanted on a scheme
of painted pleasure; when life is half
gone he begins to discern his error, and
the residue steals away in repentance, and
the profitless acquirement of a too late
experience.

I fear my Wiemar this language may
not be pleasing to you; you will consider
it as dictated by cold philosophy, and intended to damp your ardent hopes. No,
I desire not to damp, but to temper them,
let them diffuse over your prospects a
chastened light, but let them not dazzle
you with too vivid effulgence. Should
they vanish—should they leave you, what
a frightful desert would life appear to you!
how dark, how dreary the scene around

you! The angel who now embellishes
your fairy paradise, may be all she seems,
but what—think me not cruel—if her
heart should be *another's!* Do not so absolutely fix your soul on any one object
in existence, examine your path, rush
not blindly on; the happiness which one
has not dared to expect or hope for, is ever
the greatest when obtained, but the reality of anticipated bliss seldom, if ever,
oh! my Wiemar equals the conception.

I trust in the excellence of thy nature
that thou wilt do justice to me, that thou
wilt appreciate my counsel by the motives which influence it, and believe that
the purity and sincerity of my friendship
for thee, would be outraged if I flattered
thee in thy delusions. I will expose to
thee the flowery path of danger, and direct thee to that which though less seducing, is safer. True friendship disre-
gards selfish considerations, and rather

risks to offend by endeavouring to serve, than aims to please by concurring in what is injurious; there is no truer criterion of a friend than this. That parent does not sincerely love his child, who to avoid paining him for an instant, by reproving him when he is wrong, does him eternal injury in permitting him to retain the impression that he is right. It is as though he should suffer him to swallow poison, rather than save him by rudely dashing the cup from his lips. I will not be unto thee this weak doting parent—I will love thee, but I will be firm, and study thy good equally, at least with thy pleasure. Adieu, dearest Wiemar, impart to me all thy movements; thou canst have of thy safety no guardian more faithful than thy Rozendorf.

[*Note.* AS no letters appear in this

work, but such as are materially necessary to the elucidation of the history, the
correspondence which here ensues between
Count Wiemar and his friend, Baron Rozendorf, relative to the progress of the acquaintance of the former with Julia de
Montalban, his increasing passion for
her, and determination to make her his
wife, are omitted. It will be sufficient to
observe, that obtaining the object of his
love, Count Wiemar continued to reside
in Switzerland for the space of four years,
at the end of which period, Madame de
Montalban, (the mother of his wife,)
dying, he returns to Vienna, from which
epoch the history is again taken up.]

LETTER XIV

COUNT DARLOWITZ TO BARON ROZEN-DORF.

Lintz.

I HAVE received a letter from Wiemar, who informs me that, in consequence of the death of his wife's mother, he is preparing to quit the delightful spot where he has passed four of the most delicious years of his life. His first visit will be to Vienna, he makes no mention of intending one to me; but if he desires to embrace me as ardently as I do him, he will not very long delay conferring on me that happiness. Are you not all anxiety to behold the dear fellow? Married, Rozendorf—how say you now, with this example before your eyes? If you longer persist in your frigid resolutions to live single, I must give you up as incorrigible.

What will you think if the wife of Wiemar too help " to rescue her sex from their insignificance?" Should you find that contrary to your belief and expectation, there are two women in the world eminently good and virtuous, perhaps you may not absolutely then despair of meeting with a third, and surely, the fair she who could gain a Wiemar's love, *must* be of a superior order of beings.

His conception of what woman should be, I know is refined to romantic excess; he is all high-souled purity and delicacy in his ideas of the sex. He would have them as the Houri's of the Mahomedan paradise, the reward of the blessed. I expect from you a description of her who could fascinate such an enthusiast. Can she be any thing like my Amelia?—no,

VOL. I.   G

there is not *her* equal in existence; each day more firmly convinces me that she is peerless; nature could not produce at the same period, another. like her.

When first I became enamoured of her I was little more than twenty. Though I could not then conceive the thousandth part of the value of the jewel I coveted. I loved her by inspiration, as it were, and *felt*, rather than *discerned* her excellence. I had nothing assuredly but my ardent and unceasing affection to give me any claim to her attention; I knew myself unworthy of her, yet she became mine, and at twenty-two I was the happiest, the most blest of created beings. Amelia was but nineteen; we have already been married ten years, and I swear that from the period of my union with her to the present hour, she hath never caused me a single instant of pain, vexation, or uneasiness. Would she could say thus of me, but alas! too often, I fear have I committed error, too often grieved that delicate and susceptible mind,—but never voluntarily, no never voluntarily indeed, and never have I read reproach in the gentle looks directed towards me; always the mildness and sweetness of an angel. It is therefore I say, Amelia is unequalled, because perfect as she is, she is forbearing and lenient to the faults of others.

May Wiemar be happy in his choice; I please myself with the idea that when he is tired of Vienna he will come to Lintz—that you, rather than remain apart from us will accompany him, and that thus embosomed in this sweet retreat, we shall take pleasure in recalling to mind the incidents of our early youth, the tender and ardent friendship we entertained for each other, and in mutually enjoying our present happiness. The

Countess Wiemar will find in my Amelia one who will love her as a sister, for her who could inspire Wiemar with love cannot be undeserving of her affection.

We shall form a delightful society in the midst of retirement, we shall be the world to each other; we shall not envy those who can find their only happiness in a joyless, uninterested, and uninteresting crowd, the crowd who assemble for amusement, separate with indifference, and hear of your misfortunes, or death, without regret.   Adieu my friend—fail not to inform me when Wiemar arrives at Vienna.

LETTER XV

BARON ROZENDORF TO COUNT WIEMAR.

Vienna.

WIEMAR arrived here about eight days ago accompanied by his wife and two lovely children, a boy and girl. He appears perfectly happy, and she who has rendered him so, must as you observe, be a superior creature. With such a noble soul, so refined and delicate a mind as he possesses, no common woman could have attracted or made an impression on his heart.

You would have me describe the Countess Wiemar to you, but from my own judgment in so short a time I can tell you nothing; my opinion of her is formed entirely on her having been the choice of

our friend; as such, I must naturally conceive her to be as perfect as woman can
be, and to possess all those lovely qualities
that exalt, 'and make a beautiful female
assimilate to an angel.

With respect to her person I might be
more fortunate if accuracy of description on such a point were material. There
is nothing however in her exterior to lay
claim to extraordinary admiration. She
possesses a fine animated countenance,
her figure is delicate, yet well proportion-
ed, and there is an innocent freedom and
gracefulness in her manner that powerfully interests and bewitches.

But you must not expect from me, my
dear friend, the glowing description of
one enamoured; the charms of the fair
are best praised by him who has most
felt their power;—ask the *lover* for a
description of his *mistress*—none should

presume to form an estimate of beauty which has possessed for him no attractions.

Towards Wiemar she is all softness and tenderness, and repays his attention by the grateful demonstration of being fully sensible of it. This aimiable softness is of itself sufficient to make a man idolize his wife—for what are the most rigid virtues, what the finest qualities of the mind, the most transcendent genius in a wife, if she want that chief, most endearing, most delightful of all attractions—tenderness for her husband ?

The fair Julia is the descendant of a noble but unfortunate house ; from the age of ten years she has lived in the utmost seclusion with her mother in the canton of Zurich in Switzerland. Their little cottage was distant from any other in the valley in which they resided. Pride

made the Baroness de Montalban abandon a world, where she could no longer
appear but in poverty, and it was with
the utmost difficulty that Wiemar gained
the permission so necessary to him, to
visit her.

Julia de Montalban, lovely, innocent,
unseen, unknown, almost unprotected, was
precisely the object formed to attract his
sensible and enthusiastic soul. Forcibly
struck with her situation, and with the
idea of what it must become after the
death of her mother, already far advanced
in years, he felt an interest and compassion
rising in his breast, which gave birth to
the first sensations of tenderness for her—
a tenderness with him the offspring of the
most virtuous emotions. His soul recoiled
from the thought of dishonour—the pity
he felt was not of that humiliating description which emboldens the proud libertine to imagine that a female so cir-

cumstanced, must be flattered in becoming the object of his ruinous pursuit; his was the more generous sentiment of desiring to elevate to a sphere worthy of her, the woman he was not ashamed to love; to make her his wife in the face of the world, whom his heart had homaged in the shade.

With that noble frankness, and at the same time with that delicacy which accompanies every thought and action of our Wiemar, he solicited of the Baroness de Montalban the hand of her beloved daughter. The Baroness took only a short time for reflection; could she be otherwise than sensible of her happiness in obtaining such a protector for her child? one condition only accompanied her consent —it was, that during her life-time Wiemar should not deprive her of the society which for such a number of years had formed her only consolation, and that the

retired spot they occupied should still
continue to be their place of abode :—
against returning into society, the Baroness was unalterably fixed.

Possessed of his Julia, all places were
alike to Wiemar—he made no scruple of
yielding to the condition exacted, and,
purchasing a cottage as near as possible to
that of the Baroness, but upon a larger
plan, he established himself the happy
monarch in the midst of his little family,
and willing to become for life an inhabitant of those sublime solitudes, where he
had discovered such a mine of bliss.   But
he was not doomed to be for ever separated from us : for near four years this
fair stranger, who had robbed us of our
friend, held him captive in her native
wilds—for how much longer a period her
power might have extended, is uncertain,
when the death of the Baroness de Montalban interrupted the happiness they had

so long enjoyed—a happiness which Wiemar enthusiastically describes to have attained the uttermost point of earthly perfection; his ardent imagination can conceive nothing beyond it—" Even the first
pair in Paradise, were not more blest than
we were," said he to me. But, after the
death of her mother, Julia became incon-
solable; she shed torrents of tears, she sat
for hours by the side of her grave, and
scarcely could the entreaties of her husband
or the sight of her children, withdraw her
from it; Wiemar, alarmed, almost distracted at her intense grief, determined to
remove her as speedily as might be from a
spot where every object, and every occurrence, served to keep in mind her loss,
and renew her sorrow. He hastened his departure from Switzerland; but necessary
as this step appeared, and was, it almost
rent the heart of Julia to comply with it.

The first day of her arrival here, she

appeared so depressed and miserable, as to make it impossible to behold her without pain; tears started momentarily to her eyes, and more than once she quitted the room to shed them in secret.—I can conceive the sad ideas which crowded on her mind; she beheld herself in a gay and populous city, in the midst of a land of strangers, and she thought of Switzerland—and of her mother in the silent grave. I was sad, from sympathy in her sensations, and did not long oppress her with my company. I left her sacred sorrows for the tender consolation of her husband, and the soft endearments of her children; for, though my heart overflowed, I was still a stranger to her.

Wiemar is resolved that she shall go into company—that she shall dissipate, and be continually engaged in plans of amusement, till her grief has passed away, and she has regained her former state of

mind ; for naturally, he says, she possesses a great share of vivacity. Such indeed, usually accompanies innocence, and
health, and freedom from the trammels
of hypocrisy and reserve, imposed by
what is called the world.

————

IN CONTINUATION.

THE Countess Wiemar is rapidly recovering her cheerfulness. She is already infinitely courted by all who have
become acquainted with her; Wiemar
has introduced her to most of the families of distinction here; by his friends she
is generally admired : indeed it is scarcely
possible for any one to behold her without being prepossessed in her favour.
Though I still do not consider her a beauty, I allow that she is perfectly fascinating. Some of her own sex find fault with

her however, and criticise her for that
very originality, and artless grace of manner which appears to me so charming.
But the lovely sex have no severer judges
than themselves ; they are lynx-eyed to
each other's imperfections, and their fair
bosoms are a petty state of jarring sensations, where ambition and envy bear
down all before them. While the women
affect sometimes to smile at the interesting Julia, they would be glad to resemble
her—they all profess the highest wish for
her acquaintance and friendship—among
the foremost is the Countess Appollonia
Zulmer !

Appollonia Zulmer ! I hear you exclaim. Yes, my friend, even so ; but re-
collect that several years have elapsed
since the circumstance which her name
awakens in your memory. 'Tis true, she
then sought to have it believed, that Wiemar was seriously inclined towards her ;

but whether she believed it herself, admits at least of doubt. Intoxicated with his admiration, she wished him to declare himself her lover, but the admiration of Wiemar was the result of her splendid talents and accomplishments, which commanded a more than ordinary portion from most men. In no instance, if I may be allowed the expression, did his heart touch hers. She mistook, or affected to mistake, the mind, the character, of our friend, which could never assimilate with her own: she was beautiful and engaging, but she had not soul. Nevertheless, her expectations of some declaration on the side of Wiemar became obvious to him—distressed at the sentiments he had unconsciously excited, and at the ideas the Countess Zulmer permitted herself to entertain, he saw himself under the painful and embarrassing necessity of undisguisedly avowing the true state of his feelings with respect to her.

How the fair Appollonia *really* felt upon receiving this explanation from him
she had arrogated as her lover, I know
not, but certain it is, that her conduct
on the occasion, deeply affected his generous and noble soul ; from that hour she
awakened in his breast a new sentiment—
a sentiment superior to any he had before
experienced for her; she awakened his
esteem, and he became the friend of the
woman who had failed to inspire him with
love. He considers Appollonia Zulmer
as possessed of a superior mind, and of an
elevated turn of thought. He encountered her accidentally at an assembly, in
company with his wife; it was impossible
to avoid noticing her, had he even wished
to do so, but her demeanour was such, as
to set him perfectly at rest, and even call
from him an additional tribute of respect
and admiration. Any hesitation, any
embarrassment he might have experienced from the necessity there existed in this

mixed society, of introducing his wife to
her, she compleatly obviated by the delicacy and ease of her manner. The admiration, the interest she appeared to feel
for the fair Julia, was highly gratifying to
the heart of Wiemar, and naturally
heightened every disposition in her favour.
Julia too, is fascinated with the brilliant
powers of this extraordinary woman, her
wit, her elegance, her engaging conversation—she speaks of her with enthusiasm, as the most attractive female she has
yet seen. " She is like a bright star,"
said she to me, " shedding sparkling
coruscations around." I smiled at her
vivacity, and made no reply; but in
truth I am not so ardent an admirer of
the Countess Appollonia as many others;
neither am I clear, that with the same
unsuspicious generosity as Wiemar, I
should have permitted her to associate
with my wife.

Call me cynical, severe, if you will; but I believe it to be a settled principle in womankind, *never cordially or sincerely to forgive the man who has been so unfortunate as to slight their charms, or who has had the temerity to avow indifference in return for love.* It is quite otherwise with man—he is seldom, if ever, vindictive against the woman he has been *once* attached to. If she cannot repay his passion, she may *pain* but does not *irritate* him. He feels a sensible grief, which he cherishes in secret, which too often blights the fairest prospects of his future life, and hastens him to an untimely grave.

But man has more pride, and more fortitude than woman; he strives to hide from the public eye, the deep, the silent sorrow of his soul. A man will almost always entertain a tenderness for the female he has once loved; by a refined and noble gradation of sentiment, of which their little vanity renders women incapable, he will pass from the lover to the friend: he can feel no bitterness against her, but will exult in an opportunity of rendering her service at any future period of her existence. She appears to him to possess a claim on his heart, from having once agitated it with the profoundest emotion. Woman, on the contrary, harbours *vengeance*. She begins to *hate* from the moment she ceases to *love*, and her tenderness is at an end the instant her *vanity* is outraged. Between these two extremes of passion, she knows no medium.

" How harsh these censures," I hear you exclaim; but remember, my friend, I speak not of superior beings, such as your Amelia, only of the general character of the sex, and I must retain my opinion, that it is better to provoke a fierce hyena, than to excite a *woman's rage*.

When your favourite Ovid painted in such glowing colours the savage Bacchanals in their frantic orgies, when giving a loose to their wild furor, they murdered the tuneful Orpheus, he did it from a knowledge of the revengeful character of the sex; it was a happy illustration of his secret opinion of them, and you will allow no one could have better opportunities of knowing them, than this famed poet of the Augustan age.

IN CONTINUATION.

THE Countess Zulmer endeavours to prove my opinions erroneous and unjust; one would almost believe from her conduct that she suspected them, that she read them in my looks, and resolved to make me recant them. Can it be indeed possible that this triumph shall belong to her?

the female in the world, whom of all others, I should have looked to for a confirmation of them. She is almost the shadow of the Countess Wiemar, she appears to regard her with the interest, the tenderness, and affection of a sister; nor is it only when in her society that she seems so impressed with admiration for her—in every company I enter, if there be any among them who have not yet seen Julia, I am sure to hear of the glowing description which the Countess Zulmer has given of her loveliness, her enchanting manners, her various graces and attractions.

As the fair Appollonia is reckoned the standard of female taste in Vienna, every one considers her approbation as the test of perfection, and is eager to behold the object who has so powerfully excited it. Can it be possible, I must again ask, that she *really* experiences these sentiments in her favour? *Can* she sincerely, and unre-

servedly, regard the *wife of Wiemar?* of the
man, whose wife she herself once hoped
to have become? Can she really love
the woman he has avowedly *preferred* to
herself? If so, she is indeed a rare exception to my doctrine—she must, as
Wiemar conceives, possess a mind singu-
larly elevated and noble; her soul must
be of the most generous and heroic cast,
and I am prepared, if she convince me of
her truth, to do homage at her feet for
my suspicions!

Wiemar considers it would be the most
harsh and unwarrantable cruelty to debar
her from the society of his wife; he thinks
too that Julia herself would regret it—her
wit, her vivacity, her pleasing converse,
help to draw her more effectually than almost any thing, from the melancholy in
which she is still frequently plunged; she
has absolutely won the heart of Julia, and
Wiemar trusts to the natural bent of her

character, her sense, and discernment, to draw the line between *admiration* and *imitation*. " I admire the Countess Zulmer," said he to his wife in my presence, " I admire her equally, perhaps, with you— in some respects you may even esteem her, but love her you cannot, for she is not made to be loved.— She has a rare *assemblage*, but not a *union* of fine qualities; she has more dazzling accomplishments than solid ones, and her character is so various, there is no point, as it were, round which affection could rally. She is formed rather for the world at large than to embellish the domestic circle. Her brilliancy, like the lustre of the glow-worm, which, when secluded, perishes, can exist only while it is widely diffused—to attempt to concentrate, and bid it shine on the tranquil path of private life, would be to destroy it.

Such are the sentiments Wiemar delivers of Appollonia. " And why, then," said I to him, one day when we were alone, " why suffer your wife to associate with one you would not wish her to resemble? Why put her to the imminent risk of admiring one you would not have her imitate ? Is there not somewhat of inconsistency, if not imprudence, in this, my dear Wiemar.

" No !" said he with quickness, " there is no risk ; the points of difference in the character of each are so strong, that it is morally impossible they should ever assimilate; as well could Appollonia acquire the virtues and softness of Julia, as Julia the animation and bold independence of Appollonia. Nature formed them in different moulds; they may associate with as little danger of combination as any two opposites in existence."

" A man," said I, " will cautiously

select the *male* acquaintance he admits to his house, but he is often too indifferent with respect to the *females*. I am of opinion the corruption of woman is chiefly attributable to woman; if man sometimes *avails* himself of it, *woman* lays the first seed."

" Strong language, my friend," observed Wiemar; " you do not, I trust, apply its full bearing to the Countess Zulmer."

" I should be unjust to do so," I replied, " as I am not sufficiently acquainted with her *real* character—I have heard she gave her husband great uneasiness—nay, more, that her conduct shortened his life."

" Ungenerous reports," said Wiemar, " will often exist against a woman who is beautiful, and whose manners are unre-

served, yet we should judge what credit
to attach to them, when she is well received by society, whose sanction gives
the lie to calumny."

"She is well received, certainly," I
replied; "she is even courted—"

"True!" said Wiemar, in an animated
voice, "and I would not degrade *my wife*
so much as to suppose, that a female well
received by all the world, could be *dangerous for her alone.*"

I had not a word to say; I looked at
Wiemar—his fine eyes sparkled with a
noble pride—I pressed his hand in silence.

Julia presently joined us, wholly unconscious of what had been the subject
of conversation: how beautifully did she
seem to justify the confidence of her hus-

band. Though her figure is delicate, the
majesty of virtue made it at that moment
appear sublime. She towered in innocence, and a graceful dignity shone in
her looks. Heavens! how superior the
mild light of her charms, to those of
painful brilliancy which dazzle in an Appollonia. Would she were at Lintz with
your Amelia.

The world, that is, the world of Vienna, declares the Countess Zulmer to be
grace and elegance itself—the women
openly express their admiration of her, as
if they hoped, by doing so, to extort a
portion for themselves for their magnani-
mity at least, if it be refused to their
charms; but the world is very weak—no
one is bold enough to disclaim universal
suffrage. The Countess Zulmer is well
received by the *world* because *individuals*
want fortitude. Besides, few have cou-

rage to examine too closely what gives
them pleasure; they shut their eyes rather than behold the truth. Content in
deriving entertainment, they are not
over scrupulous with respect to the
means. The moment Appollonia appears, the dullest party is enliven-
ed. Frigid matrons, and women of
profound virtue, who by the bye are not
always remarkable for the profundity of
their intellect, are delighted in her society.
Purity of principle, and the utmost virtue,
unless accompanied by a certain strength
of mind, will not empower women to find
resources in themselves, nor prevent them
from resorting to extraneous means of
relieving time, which they feel burthen-
some. Hence these dignified females
simper at the approach of the Countess,
who like a fair Euphrosine, advances towards them—the goddess of mirth and
smiles. She knows how to humour every
one; and while people believe they are

pleased with her, it is with themselves that they are pleased, for she has flattered their self-love in the most delicate and artful manner imaginable.

Now, I would ask, is it not difficult to be so fascinated by the externals of a dangerous character, and yet fix bounds to feelings?—Is it possible to say, thus far will I allow myself to go and no further? Thus much is admirable, all else must be shunned? No, the gradation of sentiment is too imperceptible to be guarded against. Where we admire, we approve; where we approve, how easily do we love! Can we, then deem inexcusable the faults of those we regard?—We endeavour to palliate, to lessen them; we become reconciled, and conclude by adopting them.

I aver it—such a woman as Appollonia Zulmer is calculated to do more mischief to her sex than the most abandoned libertine of ours, the most avowed profligate of her own. She is an enchantress—a Circe ; and her arts enable her to conceal her deformity under the mask of the most seducing beauty.

Farewel! when Wiemar is weary of the frivolity of the capital, and considers that the Countess is sufficiently restored to herself to bear the seclusion of the country, he will pay thee a visit.

LETTER XVI.

THE COUNTESS APPOLLONIA ZULMER TO
MADAME DE HAUTVILLE.

Vienna.

WHO do you think, my dear gouvernante, is returned once more within my magic circle?—My heart so overflows with joy and exultation, I can scarcely tell you.—Guess, if you can; rack your brain, and give it up in despair, as I a thousand times have given up all hope. Yes—*he* is again in Vienna!—not a quarter of a mile from my habitation. —Who?—why the perfidious Wiemar! "Returned!" methinks I hear you exclaim; " dare he again shew his face so near you?—dare he appear in your presence?" He dare—and what is more, ac-

companied by a wife! At this I see my
dear gouvernante lift up her hands and
eyes, and wonder at my exultation, which
she begins to imagine the effect of frenzy! Be not alarmed however, I am perfectly sane, yet I exult!—oh! yes I triumph.—not because I love the traitor
still, or because I have again an opportunity of beholding him—no, I would wi-
ther him with a look—I would blast him
if my eyes could do it!—But because he
comes, like the devoted lamb, he comes
for sacrifice! he stoops his head, wreath-
ed with the flowers of love and joy, for my
revenge! Let me stay my uplifted arm,
while faithful memory nerves and collects
into it all the strength of my soul—let
me call before me that fatal night, when
mad with my passion for him, when intoxicated by his lovely presence, by the
tender softness of his eyes, his manners, I
fancied that I read love struggling with
timidity. Let me call to mind, how for-

getful of myself, of my native pride and dignity, I condescended, wretch that I was, to avow my feelings—to avow the love he had inspired! Oh! shall I ever forget how that-countenance, a moment before so sublimely animated, so expressive of tenderness and passion, became o'ercast! how the loves and graces that sat on his brow vanished, and gave place to confusion and terror, as though suddenly he had perceived himself in the trammels of a Calypso! how his freezing manners bore testimony to the coldness of the heart which dictated them—Ah! distraction! Why do I dwell on the maddening recollection? Was I not despised! rejected!—treated with contempt! Can I ever forget that moment—that moment that covered me with indelible disgrace!— Oh! no, no. For long, I swear it to thee, I never retired to rest, I never arose, but this horrible moment was still present to my mind; I was still an actor in the hateful scene—and with cruel faithful accuracy, imagination writhed on the points which made my degradation most complete. I felt myself a wretch, lost, plunged in degeneracy from which nothing could ever extricate me but adequate revenge. Without this I acknowledged that the devotion of the whole sex could never retrieve me.

Often, when surrounded by the flattering crowd of fools, I have conceived myself like some arch impostor, some mockery of my former self, receiving homage not my due. Oh! the pangs I suffered! and shall he then escape? No; he who felt not for a heart smarting under the tortures of despised love, shall be paid *in kind*—have I not said so? He had no mercy, neither will I. He shall learn what it is to love, to adore, and to be *spurned!*—to place his hopes, and meet disappointment! In the very *heart* and *core* of his security will I introduce the scorpion that shall sting him to madness! Yes, the fiat has gone forth—I have pledged and bound myself to his perdition, and till I have atchieved it, I cannot, no, I cannot be retrieved in my own eyes.

Now I begin to emerge—I behold at a distance the talisman which is to end the spell of my disgrace ; I will seize, I will grasp it with a hand of iron. *Deep*, and sweet as deep, shall be my revenge.

Oh! how I at once adored and hated the wretch for presenting himself to my view ; adored him for coming to deliver himself to my vengeance, yet hated him for meriting it. What power must the artful smiles of the seducer have once possessed over my soul, for his presence even now to excite in me the most turbulent, the most opposite sensations.—But let me endeavour to be methodical and calm—I wish, if I can, to give you some account of my commencing operations.

No sooner, then, did I learn that the insolent Wiemar had presumed to return to Vienna, than I own to you I felt a most sensible and violent emotion. When I heard that he was married, I will not deny that my indignation rose to a suffocating height. Soon however, quelling every weakness of the heart, I considered that by such a step he had bound me down as it were—that he had made an added and imperious call on me to revenge his aggravated insults, and I have told you that I have solemnly pledged myself to do so.—Know you how solemnly? Falling on my knees before my crucifix, I swore that no obstacle should intimidate me that I would not shrink, but deaf to the voice of pity or remorse, pursue him to destruction! Thus have I leagued religious obligation with the execution of my vengeance, and imposed on myself a sacred necessity for its performance.

What think you, my dear gouvernante, of this? You will tell me, perhaps, that I am deceiving myself, and that conscious of my weakness, I have endeavoured to guard against the operation of my pity for one I do not sufficiently detest, that I have doubted my resolution, and the inflexibility of my heart. All this you will probably say, but no matter—let time be my evidence: you will find I have turned bigot in the cause of my revenge. Have not fanatic and ambitious tyrants hunted even unto death those who would not acknowledge their sovereignty? Have they not bound themselves by oath to persecute, to torture? They have raised the standard of religion—they have rallied round it, and the profession of a different faith hath been the signal for destruction.

Well then, make the application. Wiemar—has he not rebelled against my sovereignty—and shall I spare him?

———

My soul calmed by its settled purpose, I became curious to observe what line of conduct my hero would adopt; would he seek me or avoid me? How would he act? He came not near me—he endeavoured to shun me, or I fancied so, for he was never in any society of which I was one.—Oh! most politic Count! And wherefore was this? for, when last we parted, did we not as *you fully believed* part in highest friendship? Did you not assure me of your unceasing esteem—of your admiration? Did I not let you escape, poor struggling captive as you were? Why then this want of gratitude, this audacious disrespect? Why by each act of thine wilt thou add a lash to the scourge I hold over thee?

Three weeks nearly elapsed, and I had not yet encountered him. I became impatient, for it was necessary that I should see him and be introduced to his wife. I determined two days more should not elapse ere I gained my will. I waited upon the old Baron von Esch; with him and his antiquated spouse I can do just as I please, for without the happiness of my company now and then they could not exist. I therefore made myself more than commonly agreeable to them, and artfully engaged them to send a formal invitation to the Count and Countess Wiemar. I had not much apprehension of the invitation being refused, for I had heard that Wiemar went much into public and frequented society for the purpose of amusing the melancholy of his wife, who has recently lost her mother. After

being obliged to hear much idle remark upon the long absence, marriage,
and unexpected return of Count Wiemar,
besides a long string of heavy observations on subjects the most uninteresting
(the price I paid for having gained my
point)—I was suffered to take my leave.

I had displayed much generalship during my stay, having made it appear to
the good souls as if I was wholly indifferent to that which was the real purport
of my visit, and that I had merely proposed the invitation to the Count and his
Helvetic bride, with a view to their gratification, well knowing their silly vanity
and idle curiosity, which last was powerfully excited to behold the wife of Wiemar.

In the course of the following day, I
called in *by chance*—casually led to the
subject on which I wanted information,

and heard with no small degree of pleasure, that they were expected on the day
appointed to entertain them. The Baron
Rozendorf had been included in the invitation by these over busy ideots, who,
going beyond my intention, thought they
could do no less than ask the most inti-
mate friend of the Count to accompany
him. I hate that man, that Baron Rozendorf—his dark severe eye looks you
through. His brows for ever knit—his
cynic smile—his cold unbending air sufficiently mark his character ; always mus-
ing too—always diving into motives,
watching events, and calculating results.
I felt a sudden damp, for I knew his presence would operate as a check on me for
the evening.

Well then, not to keep you in suspense,
the evening arrives—the momentous evening on which I am to behold, face to face,
him I so dread, yet long to see. I attire my-

self with studied, yet graceful negligence, and go early that I may be there before Wiemar, and before the rest of the company begin to throng in. Good Heaven! how many uninteresting faces was I obliged to see ere that for which I eagerly sought! —how many a vacant eye did I encounter in my anxious gaze for those two brilliant stars which were to flash defiance at me. Every time a carriage rolled into the court I felt extraordinary emotion, and when it proved not to have been Wiemar's how angry was I with myself. Every time the door opened I looked towards it with a palpitating heart. At length—a face, a figure presents itself—oh! of what a superior race of beings to the wretches I had been doomed for the last half hour to behold, did the perfidious too charming Wiemar appear!—that noble air, that graceful form that might have served a sculptor for Apollo! that eye like mighty Alexander's languishing yet commanding, again, after a lapse of more than four years, met my view. Ah! what an object for vengeance!—what pity!—yet what pride to immolate him! Pity! what, said I? Yes, he met my view—after those cruel insults—after his base ingratitude and scorn—he met my view, accompanied by a—wife! Let me dwell on that picture, let me think of the effect produced—when I beheld beside *him* who had scorned the love of Appollonia *another whom he dared prefer to her!*—need one have a vindictive heart to take revenge for this?

When he first entered the room he did not perceive me,—as soon as I had heard his name announced—(an instant sufficed for a glance) I purposely averted my head, and with apparent earnestness began conversing with an old dowager beside me, that I might seem as if I had been too deeply engaged to have observed

him, or to have attended to the mention
of his name even. As I heard, I should
have said *felt* the lovely youth approach-
ing to that part of the room where I sat,
I suddenly turned round and transfixed
him with a look! Yes, I protest to you,
Wiemar was transfixed, but presently recovering himself as he beheld the cast of
my countenance, (for I thought a melancholy softness, animated by a tender shade
of pleasure, would become me best,) he
drew near, and paid me some handsome
compliments with a delicacy that might
have softened a less angry spirit than
mine. While he was addressing me I
looked towards his wife with an air such
as compelled him to say, though not,
perhaps, without some embarrassment,
" May I have the honour of introducing
to you the Countess Wiemar ?"

I bowed with as much grace as I could
assume. " I shall indeed be most hap-

py," I replied; and putting forth my hand to the fair creature he presented to me, I added, " let me indulge the hope, that I may be favoured with her acquaintance and *friendship.*"

If a slight cloud had overcast the brow of Wiemar, it now completely disappeared, and he looked at me, I thought, at once pleased and gratified. Yes, those sweetly rebellious eyes once more shone with pleasure as they looked on me, and conveyed to my heart—I own it—a thrilling emotion ! The Countess absolutely seemed to view me with a feeling of admiration. She curtsied with the most winning and graceful air you can conceive, and instantly seated herself beside me. Wiemar conversed a few moments round the circle, and then came and took his seat next us. We were all three speedily engaged in a conversation which assumed by degrees a character of interest in proportion as it became more unreserved.

What a situation, my dear preceptress, for your Appollonia!—seated between the man she had fondly loved, and the woman he had preferred to her,—conversing with them even on the most interesting topics, and while she shook internally with strong contrasted feeling, appearing as tranquil, and as unembarrassed. as if her heart had been wholly dead to the past, or as if it had never occurred.

In order to preserve my composure, I avoided as much as possible looking towards *one* part of the room—it was that where, like a gloomy uneasy ghost, sat the Baron Rozendorf; from time to time, however, my eyes unavoidably met his ungenial glance, and uniformly I observed his dark brows to knit. Why should that man's watchful gaze pursue me?—he has no motive for suspicion against me that I know of; be it as it may, the recesses of *my* heart are as deeply hidden from him as they are from others; he cannot pierce them with his eyes or thoughts, and I do not fear him.

IN CONTINUATION.

THE Baron Rozendorf could not prevent me from ingratiating myself most completely with the Countess Wiemar, ere the company separated. I assure you I did wonders for a beginning. I must in honour confess, it is impossible not to admire the choice of the rebel Wiemar; there is a something in the lovely Julia irresistibly fascinating; the very creature for him, so gentle, so diffident—a perfect sensitive! Yes, these are the spiritless qualities for him. He is unworthy of a woman of superior stamp—of a towering genius, of a soaring, independent soul. Wiemar, I am now certain, could never tolerate greatness in a woman; no extraordinary powers,—no boldness of mind—greatness with him would be an unpardonable crime. He must have gentle softness! blandness—sweet imbecility! acknowledged dependance. Degrading characteristics!—contemptible graces! and contemptible those who can be attracted by them. Arbitrary tyrant! man! —if such be the better means of charming you—may I *never* charm—no, not to please a Wiemar would I become this wretch!

Yet all these soft and delicate virtues—these endearing timidities sit so well upon the Countess Wiemar, that she appears quite captivating. You see that nothing is forced—that it is not in her nature to be otherwise than she seems—that she was born, not to *lead*, but to be *led*, and tamely to yield to the destiny which marks *woman* for the *slave of man!* Horrid destiny—mine is the glory of towering above it. I could never consent to restrain a single observation that I wished to make, for fear of displeasing my assumed sovereign, or, to retract any opinion I conceived founded in reason—-or to embrace any contrary to my judgment, because, in lordly voice he declares it to be his.

The fact is, that the pride and vanity of man—in other words his *self-love* causes him to *dread superiority in woman*, he bears no rival near the throne! Why else this endless despotism? why this alarm? this unceasing watchfulness over the female mind, to arrest it in its first, least step towards knowledge if it is not from a servile dread, that their eyes should become opened!—that perceiving their equality in the scale of existence, they should (rebelling) throw off the iron yoke of slavery and never more consent to wear it! Ah! this would ill suit the despots—Like the Roman tyrants they would found their reign on ignorance and oppression, and stifle in its birth every germ of improvement.

Tame endurance is fit only for those miserable and wretched beings, who fill the seraglios of the East; the avenues to whose souls are early choaked up, and their minds contracted to the limited sphere of their future destination in existence. They are told from their infancy that they are intended for the vilest and most abject slave of man!—the idea becomes impressed as a *fate*, against which it would be vain to rebel; they submit tranquilly, they even hug their chains.

But, to return to the Countess Wiemar —ah! if my rage could slumber, the pronouncing of that name alone would be a talisman to rouse it. There is an air of melancholy diffused over her countenance, but in spite of that, you can perceive, that it is naturally a most animated one. The poor creature! I really felt compassion for her. If you could have seen the deference—yes, the deference she paid her acknowledged lord; how her sparkling eyes, ashamed, as it were, of their own brilliancy followed and waited upon his:—how invariably, if appealed to, her opinions coincided with those he expressed: if addressed exclusively on any subject, she answered hesitating with timidity, fearful, I suppose, lest she should express an idea not *perfectly* consonant with his, or lest he might disapprove it. Oh,

flattering homage from woman to man !
—instinctive adulation, which self-interest
teaches us to pay ! odorous incense! most
grateful to his soul ! How condescending!
how inestimable the approving smile he
deigns you in return !—happy slave !—
most excellent master !

And yet this woman absolutely possesses powers ; man subjects her to his
dominion among other animals, yet she
absolutely possesses powers. Yes, not-
withstanding the thick veil which habitual
oppression has cast over them, I discovered them.

But she is wholly unacquainted with
life, or with the proper exertion of those
faculties with which bounteous nature
has blessed her. Surely she will not wait
to be taught by the world, to which she
is thus late introduced, a due sense of her
own consequence and what she is capable

of. Holding, as she does, the entire happiness of an individual in her hands, she will learn her power of dispensing misery if she choose, and thus her absolute dependance will become, at least, questionable to her. She will find herself a grand link of the chain, of which she believes herself the most inconsiderable. Yet, should no female be found to take upon herself the pleasing task of enlightening her, *I* volunteer, and pledge myself to do it. No, no, fair Julia, you shall not go out of the world in your ignorance, I will initiate you! I will shew you the extent of your dominion, and how infinitely you are sovereign over the fate of him you obey. I will shew you, that if you give him happiness it is by favour, and not of necessity. The secret of your slavery must be unfolded to you. You shall taste of the tree of knowledge. Thus shall the haughty Wiemar be justly punished, and I gain my revenge.

If I am not strangely deceived, through those bewitching and timid eyes of my fair one, I discern an heart tremblingly alive to the strongest impulses of passion. That ardent cheek and animated countenance, denotes no soul insensible to the delights of love! much, indeed, do I err, if the delusions of the heart, might not lead her captive, and if reason, or even virtue, would have power to overcome the fascination of sentiment.

IN CONTINUATION.

PERSEVERANCE is the surest road to success, 'tis far better than a *coup de main*. Whoever was the plodding genius that discovered this, is entitled to my best thanks; for fully impressed am I with the soundness of the principle.

I paid a visit to the lovely Julia, two days after I had seen her at the Baron von Esch's. She received me with undisguised pleasure, which flattered me very much, and happened to be entirely alone when I was first introduced. I made good use of my time, and changed the conversation from one subject to another, for the purpose of coming at her sentiments on each, that I might be enabled to form a judgment of her character. For we subtle spirits do not require years to make ourselves acquainted with the character, which is, in fact, almost always variable, or may, at all events, be materially influenced by circumstances: we skim the surface like the sea-bird the briny wave, and we are as much acquainted with the elements as if we dived beneath.

I never, in my life-time, met with a creature so wholly artless and unaffected. She has absolutely not the smallest idea of what is *meant* by vice. It is not that she expresses a violent or rigid abhorrence of it, but that she is unacquainted with its nature. It seems as foreign to her moral notions and conceptions, as a strange and unheard of land would appear to her physical ones. I cannot describe to you her innocence and simplicity, the terms of evil, are those of a language, to her, of which she has not yet learnt the rudiments. It is astonishing to conceive, how even in the bosom of solitude, she could have preserved such unsullied and primitive purity.

After all, my dear gouvernante, this innocence is very dangerous. It is better to have some knowledge of vice, because it is not till we are acquainted with it, that we can be truly said to abhor it, or that we are even capable of shunning it. To the Countess Wiemar, it appears that every one is naturally good, and she cannot conceive how any one can be otherwise; for, ignorant of the various passions of the human heart, and of the incentives to vice, she thinks it far more natural and probable that persons should be virtuous. " For why," says she, " should any one act wrong, or do that which they feel to be so, since they must thence become unhappy, and no one voluntarily would be unhappy."

I was not long permitted to enjoy alone, society and observations so novel to me. Wiemar soon joined us, and on first entering the room, I observed, spite of his efforts to receive me graciously, that he changed colour on seeing me. How I hated him for the emotion he displayed, for do I not well know it was caused by dark suspicions of me, which rushed through his mind? Yes, yes, the coward! he knows he has not deserved well of me, and he dreads my power. I arose with an easy air and paid my compliments to him.

"Count," said I, "I have been absolutely bewitched, but it is impossible for me to break my spell; in other words, to quit her who has so enchanted me, unless you allow her to promise that she shall again, to-morrow, exercise her power over me." I had before pressed her to return my visit on the following day, but the little ideot was afraid to consent without the *permission* of her *husband*. As soon, however, as she saw from his countenance that he would not deny, she consented with eagerness.

Oh, all this is very well for a beginning, she will soon come to me, not only

without his permission, but without his
knowledge. Every thing must be pro-
gressive, it is the rule of nature. The
boy becomes a man; the acorn becomes a tree; minutes, hours, and
days, at length make up a life. Julia Wiemar will be, in time, all I can
wish.

"But what, my dear Appollonia," I hear
you exclaim, "can you possibly have
to do with the *wife* of Wiemar? Surely
it is himself alone who is the proper object of your vengeance." In answer to
your observation, permit me to relate to
you the following apologue, which I
read the other day in a book of eastern
stories.

"A certain caliph, being offended with
his grand vizier, caused his wife, whom
he knew that he passionately loved, to be
brought forth, and after having inflicted

on her the most cruel tortures, *in the presence of her husband,* ordered her to be beheaded. The same wretched tyrant being soon after offended with another of his ministers, ordered all his children, one by one, to be *murdered before his eyes.*" Ancient history furnishes us with a thousand examples, to shew that the most refined and sanguinary species of vengeance, has been that which has been taken, not on the *offending party,* but on those whom they have *prized more than life itself !*—through a *beloved bosom* has the stab been a thousand times keener, than if directed against *their own*—more painful than death itself, which would have been comparative mercy ! Can you not make the application, my dear gouvernante ?

The marriage of Wiemar (which in the confined view you take of the subject, appears to you an event calculated for ever to set my busy mind at rest) is the precise

thing which gives new vigour to my hopes
—of vengeance! It is the foundation
ready laid for me, on which I must act—
the ground on which my fabric must be
reared, for were Wiemar *not* married,
what, indeed, *could* I do? His fair wife
is the very creature that in my love, (that
is my *present* love for him) I would have
selected; she must be my *chief instrument*
in the reward my *gratitude* for his benign
friendship assigns.

But still you do not conceive! no, you
cannot, the mighty project of which I
am full; neither is it necessary that you
should. All is hatching, nothing ripe!
In *time* you shall know whatever now appears mysterious. I have the sketch in
my brain; I behold a long perspective
too, where all is regular and defined, I
see before me the path I intend to steer,
the embryo events to which I shall give
birth; their result—their consequences,

as yet involved in shadow, but of which the grand and perfect outline is discernible to my fancy! Adieu for the present, my dear friend; my spirits are exhausted —you shall hear from me soon again.

LETTER XVII.

MADAME DE HAUTVILLE TO THE COUNTESS APPOLIONIA ZULMER.

Strasburgh.

I HAVE ever heard from you with pleasure, my dear child, with but one exception, and that is when Count Wiemar has been your theme. What pain and grief were your letters wont to give me about four years ago; I saw that you were rapidly becoming entangled in the most foolish and dangerous of all passions to which the female mind can be subject—need I say, Love? I suffered my fears to be too easily tranquillized by your protestations of security, but, above all, by your having for long forborne to speak of him in your letters. Your last, however, revives that unfortunate topic, and with it my fears revive likewise. Fears? said I; I should rather have said regrets, for it is but too clear that you *still* love!—ah! start! be indignant if you will, let your piercing eyes flash flame—I repeat it; you still love! love more ardently than ever this unworthy man.

Oh! Appollonia! if you loved him not, why that trembling eagerness to behold an ingrate? why that emotion you found it so difficult to conceal when you did behold him? Had you been indifferent, you would neither have shunned nor sought him, you would have recog-

nised him without a sensation, or if with
any, one of *contempt* alone. You would
not have conceived the mere matter of his
arrival, a piece of intelligence worth communicating to me; above all, you would
not have made an *era* of it, from which to
date your operations : you would not have
considered it an event worth particulari-
zing, nor would the news of his *death*, even,
have made more than a passing impression on your mind.

This it is to be *really* indifferent, my
dear child, and indifference is more ini-
mical to love than even *hate itself*, for hate
is but a passion of the mind, which a
stronger passion may subdue, whereas indifference is the icy coldness of the heart,
which renders it dead to every impression.

Alas! how mortifying is it to me, to
find that all my lessons have been thrown

away upon you. Four years have elapsed since he quitted Vienna, consequently since you have seen him, and yet you have not forgotten him. His very name is the signal for pain and uneasiness to you. I protest, that even at your age, I never deemed any man worth five minutes consideration. I do not believe that it would have been possible for the most accomplished of his sex to have found his way to my heart; of this, at least, I am certain, he could never have given it pain. When love ceases to be pleasure, is it not the height of folly to yield to it? why should we cherish pain?

Doubtless I am incompetent to speak on this extravagant passion, which I was always too reasonable to feel, yet I am far from regretting my incapacity. Have I not always laboured to guard you against the allurements of love, against the mischief of a *real passion*? yet in spite of the shield of iron which I believed I had spread before your heart, in spite of the bulwarks by which I flattered myself, I had fortified and secured the liberty of that citadel, I find myself at this late period completely foiled, and the pupil I watched over with so much care, falls the readiest victim to all I sought to preserve her from!

What tell you me of your revenge? Appollonia! Appollonia! be not deceived, 'tis but the apology you offer to your heart, for dwelling on the image of one you feel you ought to hate. Had you not loved him to a degree far beyond what I could have supposed you capable of, another lover long since had displaced him, and he would have been consigned to the oblivion of which he was alone worthy. Call your pride to your aid my dear child, let not your reason become the dupe of an unworthy passion. Call to mind your wrongs and the insults you have received, but let them operate differently. These transports of rage savour too much of unextinguished love. When you feel your soul dissolving in tenderness, as often I know you do, I would have the thought of them rouse you, like a thunder-clap, to a sense of what you owe yourself. I have somewhere read of a philosopher, who was so apprehensive of falling into the *weakness* of sleep, that when he reposed on a couch, he held in his hand a ball of brass, which by falling into a bason of the same metal placed beneath, aroused him the instant a temporary forgetfulness crept over his faculties. This precaution, metaphorically, I would recommend to you, keep likewise a constant watch over yourself, or you will be overcome, and fall into a doting imbecile dream, from which you will find it difficult to waken.

Why was it that so ardently I pressed

you to marry the Count Zulmer? (a man, indeed, more than old enough to have been your father) why, but because I wished to emancipate you from the odious shackles of your illiberal relations, to render you your own mistress, to place you above those who conceived that the most abject humility could never repay them for their hard-wrung benevolence to you. To give you opulence and power, but, above all, early to prove to you, that the sentiment which is called *love*, was by no means necessary to happiness. You thought so, my dear Appollonia, till you beheld this Wiemar; then adieu to all those excellent lessons I had so laboured to inculcate in you! Yet it had been no matter, perhaps—you were amenable to none, save yourself; every obstacle removed, all might have been well, had your love been justly placed; but unluckily my principle, that to admit love into the breast at all is to admit a dangerous guest and a betrayer of happiness—has become too truly exemplified in you.

Love, my dear child, subverts—perhaps I should say *suborns* the understanding—deprives us of our self controul, robs us of our pride, overthrows our dignity, fills our souls with degrading jealousies, petty cares, and vain regrets. Have you not found it so ? Tell me, were you not happier before the intrusion of, and stubborn dominion of this unlucky passion ?

The poor, good old Count !—Happy to be possessed of a young and beautiful wife, he felt as much gratitude at the admiration she obtained abroad, as if he experienced all the sweets of domestic comfort at home. If you praised his wife, he thanked you as much as if you praised his taste—it was a compliment, for it amounted to the same thing, and for this, (which by the bye was the only

compensation he received for the solid be-
nefits he had conferred) you rolled in afflu-
ence, and rioted in every pleasure. The
kind creature was wisely content—had he
married a young lovely woman, in the
expectation, as M. de Hautville did, of
finding a nurse, he would have been very
properly disappointed. Oh ! if the sex
knew but wisdom—the wisdom of power
and pleasure, they would always wed old
men. A boy may be commanded, but
only for a time, he will become older, and
burst his fetters; an old man (by an in-
verse ratio) becomes every day more
humble, tractable, and subservient.

Were you not free as air when your
husband was alive, and gay as the careless
lark that proudly soars through it?—then
you were not *in love*. Now, you are the
lark confined, entangled in a net, and if
you do not struggle vigorously nothing
but death will set you free. If you are

not yet so completely bewildered by this unfortunate passion, as to have lost all care for yourself, come instantly to me, and however hopeless at this distance your case may appear to me, I will undertake in less than a month, to drive the very memory of it from your mind. If you refuse me this, it is in vain you will insist that you abhor, detest, that you burn with nothing but vengeance for this renegado! You can only prove it by flying from him. Be not within the reach of his presence. In cases such as yours, there is no remedy but precipitate flight. I tell you again, your pretence of vengeance is all a feint by which you endeavour to deceive yourself for still cherishing thoughts of him. Come to me—we will go to Paris. In the life, bustle, and variety of that charming spot—in the crowd of gallants that will surround you—in the envy of the women, and *piquant* flattery of the men, this image,

which has taken such powerful possession of your heart, will speedily be
chased thence, and what will go furthest
in compleating your cure, in all probability be displaced by another.

Adieu for the present, my dear child;
consider all I have said to you, and the
advice I have given, which cannot be
neglected without danger.

LETTER XVIII.

THE COUNTESS WIEMAR TO LADY
APPOLLONIA ZULMER.

I RETURN your ladyship many thanks for "La Nouvelle Heloise," which you have had the goodness to lend me. The story is deeply affecting, and the author, to render it so, has not scrupled to colour it most highly. It is difficult to imagine, that a sentiment, tender as that of love, and which brings with it so much happiness, could ever become a passion, violent, terrific, and productive of such misery and despair as he paints it. It is so pure a sentiment, too, yet he unites it with remorse and horror, as if *guilty love* could be a real picture. Still the improbability of this romance (and Heaven forbid it should be otherwise than improbable) does not deduct from its interest. I should be happy to rely on your ladyship's taste for the selection of some other volume.

———

LETTER XIX.

APPOLLONIA ZULMER TO THE COUNTESS WIEMAR.

YOUR ladyship received some pleasure, then, from the perusal of " La Nouvelle Heloise ;" I judged not erroneously when I conceived that your tender and elegant mind would appreciate its beauties. You think the story improbable—be assured it is less so than you imagine. *Ill-fated Julia!*—wretched St. Preux ! what heart

but must dissolve at the recital of your
sorrows ! The whole story is delineated
by the hand of a master. The characters
appear to you too highly drawn. They
are not, believe me. Unfortunately, human life can furnish a thousand in-
stances of the original : the sentimental
and sensible Rousseau knew this well.
How far beyond the pleasures of love does
he paint its pangs ! How admirable the
character of his Julia ! how refined that
of his hero ! In that instance alone,
probably he may have overcharged the
picture, for I believe there are not many
lovers to be found equally constant and
tender with St. Preux.

Since you have done me the honour
of approving my first choice, I have great
pleasure in selecting another for you from
my library, which I hope you will be
equally charmed with. This, likewise,
will forcibly interest your feelings: but,

my dear Lady Julia, I hope you are not so very unfashionable, as to call your husband to read to you while you work! In other words, I hope you do not think it *necessary* to submit every book to him for his approbation ere you venture to peruse it; your own judgment is by this time, I should conceive, sufficiently matured to direct your choice, and pure as it is it cannot err. Did he see the last I had the honour of lending you? I suppose not; it was for *your* perusal I lent it. I should select for him the more ponderous, though in his estimation, probably, the more entertaining works of ancient and abstruse authors. At all events, I take the liberty of requesting he may not behold the one which accompanies this note. Doubtless, he would not admire it equally with a more serious or learned production. It relates solely to the passions and emotions of the mind, and powerful affections of the heart—delineations in which men take no pleasure.

Adieu! my dearest Lady Julia.—Do me the favour to burn my nonsense; were it to be seen, I should be esteemed a most audacious critic upon men and books.

LETTER XX.

THE COUNTESS WIEMAR TO LADY AP-
POLLONIA ZULMER

THE BOOK RETURNED.

I MUST have the honor to return the book
which your ladyship has done me the favour to send, since you appear to think
it would not be proper for Count Wiemar
to see. Whatever is not proper for *him*
to *see* cannot be proper for *me* to *read*—
and, what I thought he could not approve
of, I should receive no pleasure in perus-
ing. I therefore do not make any sacrifice whatever in returning the book to
your ladyship, which, upon reading your
note, I deemed it not necessary even to

open. I must likewise in candour ac-. knowledge, that my husband certainly saw in my hands " La Nouvelle Heloïse," and what the observations in your note now recal to my mind, a shade of serious- ness such as was wholly new to me, overspread his countenance as he cast his eyes upon the title-page. So very foolish was I, that I never once suspected it was the *book I held in my hand,* which occasioned this momentary change; for had I thought so, I would instantly have dashed it from me. He soon resumed his usual kind looks, and slightly inquired who had lent it me. I told him you had. He then asked me, if I *approved* the work. I said it had affected me very much, and that I thought it a most interesting story. Again he looked serious, but presently with a smile asked me, if I would relinquish what I conceived so interesting, for a walk with him.

" What !" exclaimed I, " can any book be so delightful to me as your company ?" and I instantly threw it down and hastened to accompany him.

The look I received for this simple avowal of my thoughts, for it was no more, was such that Heaven knows I should have felt no regret at relinquishing for it all the books in the universe.

I have thought it proper, since your ladyship made a question of it, to put you out of doubt as to my husband's having seen the book, and I must add, that henceforth I shall submit *every* book to his inspection and approval, ere I venture to read it. I regret most deeply that for a moment I should unwittingly have given him pain or displeased him, and all the pleasure I received from the perusal of what I thought so charming, is now more than counterbalanced.

LETTER XXI.

THE COUNTESS ZULMER TO LADY JULIA WIEMAR.

WHAT a charming letter! how much do I admire your sweet simplicity! It is positively quite captivating! And did you really think me serious in my nonsense about the Count? Could you possibly believe for a single instant that I could feel the smallest hesitation in your submitting to his inspection, if you chose it, any book I might have the honour of lending you? No, indeed, my dear Lady Julia, if you thought so, you did me great injustice. I know how amiable is Count Wiemar, how liberal in his ideas, and how superior to the generality of mankind. I hope and trust your too

K 3

susceptible mind has misled you, and that you only fancied he looked serious when he found what you was reading—do not distress yourself; your sensibility has too soon taken alarm; rest assured his serious look was in your imagination alone. The Count was not, could not be displeased; his taste is too polite—his judgment too refined. "La Nouvelle Heloise," is a work too justly admired, too beautiful and sublime to displease even the most fastidious. What celebrity it acquired for its author—celebrity, said I, it has acquired him immortality! Had you gone out of the world, my dear Lady Julia, without having read "La Nouvelle Heloise," you would have lost the perusal of the most finished production that ever issued from the pen of man.

But now to convince you how completely I was in sport when I so *seriously* requested your husband might not be

permitted to see the book you so hastily
returned me, I take the liberty of sending
it you once again, and beg that you will
receive it more favourably. Deign to
open it this time at least, and if you
please, in the *presence* of your husband.
This permission, I should hope, will be a
talisman to remove every doubt and every
scruple. Adieu! I intend myself the
happiness of waiting on you very soon.
The pleasure I experience in your society, so different to any I have of late
been accustomed to, makes me most
anxious to enjoy it often.

LETTER XXII.

THE COUNTESS ZULMER TO MADAME DE HAUTVILLE.

Vienna.

NO, my dearest gouvernante, it is in vain you urge me; fly I will not from the scene of my danger, as you most erroneously deem it. What! fly from Vienna because Wiemar has arrived! acknowledge that I dread his power, his influence!—Forbid it pride, forbid it vengeance!—I will stand my ground, let *him* fly, it is for *him* to fear.

My determination fixed upon this head, I proceed to other matters. I find that I must be even more cautious than I could possibly have formed any idea of—It is so *nouvelle* to me to encounter such genuine unaffected innocence, such implicit devotion towards a husband, united to so much love;—such artlessness with such refinement of idea. Yes, my dear gouvernante, I have to encounter all these at once in the character of Julia Wiemar. I shall have a hard task with her, I find! It will require no little time and pains to draw her from her present bent, and to give her a new one. She is truly what is called virtuous; she is intrinsically what is understood by the term, and I protest to you, virtue sits so well upon her, and she appears so graceful under the burthen, that I am half in love with it, and to appear equally beautiful, could be almost tempted to take up again what I have so long cast away. But nonsense, it would sit so awkwardly upon me now, and above all things be a most troublesome companion in the prosecution of my intended operations.

I can see no fault in this little piece of primitive purity, except it be that she has *too much* simplicity. But if she is at present so simple, in time she will be otherwise. This natural gloss must wear off, and then, we shall substitute the polish of artifice. You might at this time make her credit any extravagance, provided you observed a due solemnity in the recital. Fortunately however for me, I have received a letter at the outset of my career, without which I might have taken steps somewhat too precipitate, but I shall now not fail considerably to profit by it. Having heard my fair lady express a desire for some books, I proposed to lend her as many as she chose from my own library.—She eagerly caught at the offer, but it was impossible her joy upon the occasion could equal mine, for I instantly saw the corner-stone of my foundation laid.

I know that there is not in the world a more subtle poison than that which is extracted from and administered by books. Mineral, vegetable, or other poisons, operate only on the physical system; they may destroy by sudden, violent, or gradual means, the corporeal man, but to that are their powers limited—they have none over the soul. The other, on the contrary, is the deadly poison which is slowly and involuntarily imbibed—which seems sweet and delicious, which fascinates the mental taste, and flows as a gentle though envenomed stream over a page of snow. Like honey distilling from the bee, it drops pleasure on the heart, yet, like the baleful Upas, spreads far its dangerous influence. This I say is the sovereign poison; this which affects not the body, but the mind. The soul, lapp'd in Elysium, dreams not of danger. It has no thought of the seduction which is stealing over it; no feeling which it marks for vice, no consciousness of imbibing evil. Blind to corruption, insensible to the idea of it, the mischief is not perceived till its germs having sunk, and taken root, eventually becomes revealed. Yes, this is the poison for which there is no antidote. We cannot obliterate from the mind impressions which it has strongly received. Can the thoughts which rush through the brain be recalled ? No, they are caught in their lightning flight, registered, and hung up in the gallery of memory. In vain we would erase, forget; the colours of the picture become daily more vivid, and we more deeply influenced.

Now my hope was, that the gentle Julia, young, and teeming with sensibility, would eagerly have swallowed the intoxicating draught I administered to her ; that incessantly, like a wretch in a fever, she would have raged with insatiable thirst, and called for more. ·But I have been foiled—

foiled however for a moment only; already have I more than regained the ground I lost; there is sometimes as much merit in recovering from a partial defeat, as in gaining a decisive victory.

The first book I lent the inexperienced fair one, for inexperienced she is as a child, although a wife and mother, was " La Nouvelle Heloise." With this she was charmed—I congratulated myself. " Courage," said I, this is a good beginning, for *entre nous*, there is not in my estimation a more dangerous work extant, or one better calculated for the purposes of seduction: for I defy the female, however pure in her heart, however chaste in her ideas she may be, *before* reading this book, to remain wholly unaffected, and unimpressed by its perusal. I aver that it is utterly impossible so many highly-coloured and voluptuous images as are there depicted, can be permitted to take their passage through the mind, and leave no stain behind.

The fairest snow is the easiest discoloured. Over an innocent and unvitiated mind, a book like this has most power; for on one already depraved, its delicate and elegant blandishments, would make little impression. It is well enough to *prepare the way*—to ameliorate the heart, and delude the imagination. It is vice clothed in the most seducing garb of sentiment. The tender souls who greedily imbibe it in that alluring dress, would shrink from it if presented broad and undisguised in its native—hideousness, I had almost said. When dwelling on a passage conceived in the loosest spirit, yet so combined as artfully to mislead the imagination, they believe, or endeavour to believe, that they are merely charmed with a refined or sublime idea, elegantly expressed; when the seducer, unsuspected, is hugged to the breast, he may indeed triumph in his powers of deception! Rousseau might triumph, the sentimental luxurious libertine!

For my own part I could not now derive the least gratification from books of this sort—they are mere mockery to me, though once in my turn I was fool enough to be delighted with them. I know, however, enough of the *pristine* efficacy of the one in question, to defy the fair Julia, if she peruse a score books of morality as antidotes, ever wholly to obliterate the impression she hath already received from this one. Noxious weeds, if not early exterminated, are continually springing up among the fairest flowers.

Emboldened by the success of my first essay, I ventured to cull another deleterious sweet from the same prolific garden of seduction, equal, if not surpassing the

former in its intoxicating properties—a
charming production for my purpose at
least, and worthy of the fame its author
has already acquired here. It was my
intention to have followed up this with
others of the same stamp, increasing each
time in the boldness of my choice. But
as skilful archers sometimes measure too
long a bow, I found that I likewise had
overshot my mark; and how think you?
Why, by desiring the little puritanical
soul, not to shew my book to her husband;
she took the alarm instantly; I could not
have believed her so very a simpleton,
warm, too, as she must have been from
the perusal of Heloise. I was absolutely
provoked, but as fortune always favours
the bold, and never permits them to be
wholly discomfited, I speedily rallied on
finding that my rigid piece of morality
had not even ventured to *look* on the forbidden fruit; in other words, that she had
not opened the book, which I had restrict-

ed from her husband's eyes. Can you imagine any thing to equal this?

What fine marshalling in Wiemar—what discipline, demonstrated by the submission of his wife—Ah! I should never have done for him, I see it clearly. Well, the fair slave returned my book, and as I have stated, without knowing the contents, devoid even of common female curiosity you s..—surely she must be a descendant of the stoics. The book was accompanied by a note, which I inclose for your perusal, and consequent entertainment, for certainly it is a production *unique* in its kind.

I assure you, my dear preceptress, I had no idea of such principles of passive obedience in woman;—voluntary too, not the least effort, and resulting less from a sense of duty than a feeling of pleasure. Shall this be always so? Juno! terma-

gant goddess, for our sex's honour forbid!
Forbid it laughing love!—forbid it vengeance!

How did I proceed on receiving this curious billet—this unexpected blow?—
Guess you cannot. Why simply thus:
knowing from what I had discovered of
the character of the fair one, that she
would conceive herself irremediably sullied
by the utterance of a falsehood, I had
no hesitation in fully relying on her
assertion, that she had not opened my
unfortunate book. I therefore carefully
returned it to its place on my shelf, among
its fellows, not without a latent hope
glancing through my mind, that at some
future period I should take it down again,
under more favourable auspices, for her
who had now returned it on my hands.—I
next selected one exactly resembling it in
external livery, for, in order to preserve
uniformity on my shelves, I have a certain

number, bound to correspond. This, then, I substituted, however alike in appearance, yet widely different within, treating of subjects serious, moral, and sublime. I must confess to you, I never read six pages of it myself, for I felt the horrors creeping over me as soon as I opened it. This, accompanied with a suitable letter, I sent in exchange, assuring the lady she might peruse it with safety, and that she would then become convinced there was nothing improper in it. Thus you see I gave her every reason to suppose she received the same book, and that I had but jested when I requested she would not let her husband see it.

I was favoured with a most delightful answer, which made me applaud myself for the success of my scheme—she begged a thousand pardons for her folly, and hoped I should excuse her apparent want of confidence in the propriety or excellence of my selection for her, and several pretty things to the same effect, all evincing her extreme simplicity, and want of experience.

Thus was I speedily reinstated in the good graces of the charmer. It is the clearest thing in the world, that she most earnestly desires to be upon terms of friendship with me, and where the inclination is in favour of an object, every thing is easily passed over, and readily forgotten. *This* the *men know too well,* and how to make their advantage of it.

I must, however, be on my guard in future; and before Wiemar my conduct must be of such unexceptionable propriety and exemplary discretion, as must not only retrieve, but obliterate from his mind altogether the little oversight which I have been guilty of in his estimation, and which the folly of his wife betrayed

to him.   But after all, why should I accuse myself of an oversight? for how
could I possibly foresee such an extraordinary sincerity, in woman?—such venera-
tion for, and unaffected love for *a husband!*—such implicit deference! Really,
till now, I always believed, that without
exception, the appearance of these virtues
was merely put on by unfortunate woman
in the presence of their haughty tyrants,
to soften and conciliate them, and to gain
by this little temporary restraint, such influence over them as might be requisite
for their comfort in existence, and to
ameliorate their horrid destiny. *Out of
their presence* I imagined they put them
off as easily as their garments, or as some
females do their beauty.   Even now I
hardly know how to believe the testimony of my waking reason.   I sometimes
am inclined to believe the perfect-seeming
Julia a little Machiavel of artifice; but
if so, adieu to my own boasted powers, for

she is far beyond me in the science of appearances, and I may sit down a calm spectator of her superiority.

But let me not torment myself; no, no, it is impossible, it cannot be that this mountaineer shall excel an Appollonia! Have I not genius to plan, power and inclination to execute ? Do I not hold in my hands by threads invisible, the fates of those who have offended me ? Can I not surround them many a line deep with inextricable meshes ? Can I not exert over them an influence which shall be inscrutable, because unknown and unsuspected ? Cannot I do thus ? and yet shall I degrade myself by supposing, the *she* exists who could surpass or circumvent me? Poor Julia ! it were better for thee, perhaps, were thy character less genuine. If thy heart were not so tender, or thy mind so delicately refined, thou wouldst feel less heavily the mischiefs I design

thee; but the more agonizing thy tortures, the sweeter will be the banquet of
my vengeance! Wert thou differently
organized, it would lose half its zest. Thy
sufferings would be slight, and my blows
fall heavy upon Wiemar only. Now
the same arrow which wings its poisoned
way through *his* heart, shall lay thee
too in the dust. Poor Wiemar! thou
art happy, and I would have thee enjoy all thou canst. Thou art but as a
truant school-boy, who wandering for a
day in search of pleasure, dreams not of
the punishment in store for him, and
which he must of necessity at length receive.

Bask then in the sunshine yet a-while!
Thou seest no cloud in the gay horizon
which has tempted thee to forget thy
duty; no distant thunder mutters in thy
ears; no boding flashes warn thee of a

storm before evening: No! none. It is
brooding nevertheless, and thou hast no
means of escaping. Even in thy security
shall it overtake thee.

I am now going to visit the interesting Julia; therefore, my dear preceptress,
for the present, adieu! You shall know
all my movements.

LETTER XXIII.

COUNT DARLOWITZ TO COUNT WIEMAR.

Lintz.

ARE you not almost tired of Vienna, my friend? do you not yet long for the tranquil delights of retirement? surely your fair wife by this time is no longer in need of extraneous aids to restore her cheerfulness. Come to Lintz—my Amelia, who longs to see her, our dear children and myself, will, joined by you, do our best to entertain her. We need not despair, I think, of driving the foul fiend far away from her. How cruel it is of you, Wiemar, to waste your hours in an idle town, hours which so many hearts here would delight to share with you. My eldest, Frederick, is incessantly inquiring for his godfather, Count Wiemar, and the younger children want to know when their new playfellows will arrive. Can you resist all this? and will you much longer continue to pay us so bad a compliment as to prefer, to all we can offer, the fatiguing and uninteresting amusements of the town? How anxiously I desire to see your children; five years have now elapsed since last we met; then I was, as I now am, the happy husband of the best, and most affectionate of women, the father of a family, of which an emperor might justly be proud. But you, how changed your state! I almost feared you would forswear the sex, and that as we mutually entered the vale of years, ours would never be the delightful happiness of scheming the intermarriage of our children, of living again in their rising progeny, and, like two spreading oaks, to overshadow with our branches numerous and tender scions of ourselves.

Now I again indulge the hope that my fond and favourite ideas may yet be realized ; that my ardent imagination, which in early youth so often created round me a fairy brilliant world, (presenting, as it were, a mirror to my eyes, in which I saw painted in gayest colours, the images and scenes of my future life,) has not greatly deluded me ; that her infant pencil, gifted with prescience, sketched faithfully the outlines of events to come ; and that as the morning of my existence hath already been so blessed, the evening shall set in brightness. Night, which is the tomb, shall then shroud all, but its falling shadows shall cause no terror, for we will be prepared to meet it. Is it not so, my Wiemar ? Come, and lend your aid to call into actual existence those pictured scenes of happiness which yet remain to be fulfilled. How much our dispositions assimilate,—our dispositions, only, may I presume to say, for in your character are traits so noble and sublime as mine can never aspire to. Believe me, friend of my soul, I am fully aware of my inferiority to you, and the affection you deign to feel for me, is now, as in my boyhood it was, the pride and glory of my life.

How often has the elevation of your ideas, the refined enthusiasm of your virtue, exalted me above myself; how often has your energetic reasoning, embued with all the grace and elegance of Roman eloquence, restrained me from a meditated act of folly, or stopped me short, even in its wildest career!—never committing any yourself, yet ever ready to excuse my imprudences and those of others. But although so infinitely your inferior, I had at least the merit of knowing how to value you.

For an evening, or moonlight ramble

with you, I would always give up any
pursuit, however interesting but a moment before it might have appeared to
me. - And was I not always right? for
even if improvement were my object, was
I not certain to return more edified, more
improved by one of those intellectual
rambles with you, than I could arise from
some heavy and laborious puzzler of sci-
ences, or dull lecturer on morality? Your
impassioned language—your sublime ideas
sank into my heart, and while listening
to you with inexpressible pleasure and admiration, how often have I found my
cheek wet with tears I was unconscious of
having shed. We were nearly of an age,
my Wiemar—our habits and pursuits not
very dissimilar: why may they not be as
little so now? Why, without neglect of
our duties as men, may we not renew
the habits of our early youth? Why
may not our wives form a friendship with
each other, tender and firm as our own?

Our children linked together, and our united families, like those of the patriarchs, form but one? Oh! had I the sweet tongue of a Tully, or persuasive eloquence of a Demosthenes, I would exert it now; I would move you as the lyre of Orpheus moved the trees and stones. I would lure you to us, and having *once* lured you, should have no apprehension of your quickly deserting us. I know you well enough to be assured you would rejoice in the change, and your fair wife, in lieu of the idle uninteresting follies in which she now participates, and which, I am certain, yield her no true gratification, would find herself suddenly transported into the bosom of domestic felicity. Happiness, like a heavenly calm, would gradually steal over her, and become fixed in her heart; she would soon feel the difference between pleasure which is of the soul and that which is merely ideal, and perceive that all the great world denominate such, is but a shadow of the reality.

If, after what I have said, you should still persist—but which I will hope is impossible—to remain in the town, then shall I employ an advocate, whom I am well convinced you will not think of withstanding—this advocate shall be Amelia! No, you will refuse nothing to her—that good, that excellent creature. I know the admiration and the esteem you feel for her, and well, my Wiemar, does she merit it, for where, under the cope of heaven, could thy unworthy friend have found her equal? Ah! if you knew what a being is Amelia!—you have not an idea of half her perfections—Yet perfect as she is, how forbearing, how tolerant of my faults and follies. Young as I was when she deigned to become mine, I saw, I felt, that she alone of women could make me happy—and truly did I feel, for she

has been my guide, my source of bliss
through the years we have been united.
How few, to look back on time, do those
years appear, though now almost eleven.
Ah! at the commencement of that period
how passionately I idolized her—I should
have embraced death if she had refused
to fill my arms. Now the effervescence
of my passion may have abated—but do
I idolize her less? no: more if possible—
more fervently, more deeply—a thousand
tender delicious ties are rivetted round
my heart, ties created by my union with
her; my heart is, as it were, benetted by
them, whichever way it turns, it finds
itself in an inextricable maze of love and
delight.

I behold in my fair girls, rising coun-
terparts of what their mother first appeared to me,—and in my wild boys, I
see myself—I look back on those delightful years which have passed, of which I

almost fancy I can retrace each day, so short do they appear in the retrospect. I look back and I say to myself—If I had not married Amelia, what would now have been my fate? A solitary wanderer, perhaps, over a world which would have been nothing to me. An isolated being not interested in society, and society, in in return, feeling no interest for me; a wretch, neither loved while living, nor missed, nor lamented when dead. Instead of, oh! blessed reverse! surrounded by beings who love me, to whom I am most dear—beings, the thread of whose existence is spun with mine, who cling to me —whose hearts are entwined with mine, who participate in all my joys and griefs —who give the interest, the charm to my existence, and whom, were I dying, would kneel round my bed—tenderly would close my eyes, and shed tears, bitter of regret, over my grave.

Oh! what indescribable and varied feelings! what emotions! what a distinct species of thoughts and ideas, fill the heart of him, who is embosomed in his family—who hath a lovely partner to whom he can intimately communicate his most secret sensations, and a blooming hopeful progeny centering in him their dependance, and innocent hopes.

The man who is single, is the solitary cedar of the desert; but he who is surrounded by his offspring, is the firm-rooted leafy oak, in the midst of a beauteous garden.

Think me not too great an egotist, O my Wiemar! pardon me, I know you will, you who have now began to feel the sweet emotions which inspire me with a theme that is endless. You who have now began to taste the unalloyed delight

of being a beloved husband and an ho-
noured father, you can not only pardon,
but will participate in all the overflowings
of my soul.

The scenes of the world, what pleasure
can they yield? Like the shadows of a
magic lanthorn, they pass before our eyes
without affecting our hearts. Leave then
the frivolity, idleness, and corruption of
the town, for this pure retreat. Leave
them, and try at least, if as much pleasure may not be found united only among
ourselves. Perhaps, too, your influence
may achieve more than mine ever could,
you may induce our dear Rozendorf, our
mutual friend, to join and identify himself
with us. Since he will not attempt to
form around himself a circle of domestic
happiness, of which he must be the centre, let him live in the midst of ours, and
let ours be blended in one.

LETTER XXIV.

COUNT WIEMAR TO COUNT DARLOWITZ.

Vienna.

YOU have prevailed, my dear Darlowitz. In less than a week I shall join
you, with my Julia and our children. I
read to her a part of your letter, and, delighted with the charming picture you
drew of the felicity we shall enjoy together, she eagerly exclaimed, while listening to me, " Oh ! let us be gone, my
dear Wiemar! I shall be happy, I am
sure I shall. How kind, how excellent
in you so long to debar yourself of the
pleasure of beholding such dear friends,
that I might derive amusement from the
gaieties of the town. But ah ! what su-

perior pleasure shall I experience in the
midst of those friends—yes, my heart will
indeed feel delight, which in an indifferent crowd it cannot do."

She then inquired the ages of your sweet
children, that she might compare them
with those of her own; the age, character,
and pursuits of your admirable wife, her
mode of educating her children, &c. When
I had given her as faithful a picture as I
could of her domestic life—" Oh, Wiemar!" she exclaimed in rapture, " what
a splendid example of virtue, refinement,
and strength of mind must be the Countess Darlowitz! how superior to me—
how, alas! can I ever equal her, how ever
attain her height? Let me at least hasten to become acquainted with her, that
having her constantly before my eyes, I
may endeavour to imitate her excellence,
and fashion myself on her model.

I took my lovely wife in my arms, Darlowitz. " Oh! Julia," I said, " it is for me to appreciate your virtues, and the delicacy and liberality of soul which constitute so brilliant a feature in your character! Yes, my love, Amelia is worthy to become your dearest friend, you are worthy to become her's—Let this suffice as the eulogium of both, for none can go beyond it."

"The dear children," pursued Julia, her eyes glisteniug, "how delighted each will be at the addition of the other to their party, and how much more rapid will be their mutual improvement, arising naturally out of a spirit of emulation among them when united."

" Yes," answered I, " the elder children of Darlowitz are considerably older than ours, and according to the plan of Amelia, they are her sub-teachers. She instructs them, and they transmit their knowledge to the little ones, which habit more deeply impresses on their own minds all they have learned."

"I shall adopt all the plans of the Countess Darlowitz," cried Julia with animation—"it is impossible I can do better; how happy ought I to consider myself that so admirable a model has been thrown in my path! My dearest Wiemar, how much more pleasure will you enjoy when you have a friend with whom you can *converse*, than when surrounded, as I have sometimes seen you, by persons with whom you can scarcely talk."

"Even in a crowd," answered I, "if I can but perceive my Julia, she appears to me as the sun breaking through darkness, to shed light on my soul."

"Ah! but when there are no crowds

to intervene between us—no darkness,"
she added, smiling—

" Then certainly my happiness will be,
if possible, more perfect—more resembling
that earthly paradise we enjoyed in Switzerland, among your native Alps."

At the mention of Switzerland, Julia
heaved a sigh—" My dear mother !" she
murmured, while tender tears rushed to
her eyes, and melancholy usurped for a
moment the place of her sweet smiles.
She recollected those scenes of love and
happiness at which her venerable mother
used to be present, smiling on us like a
benign protecting angel. But speedily
recovering herself, she gazed on me, then
came and threw herself into my arms, hid-
ing her face in my bosom, as though she
entreated my pardon for having given me
perchance a moment's pain,

The looks and actions of Julia are sufficiently eloquent—there is no need for her to speak. If the power of language might be easily dispensed with, it must be by her.

I have related this little scene to thee, that thou mightest form some slight idea of her whom thou wilt shortly see. Such bewitching innocence and artlessness of character, thou hast rarely beheld, and of which she has not lost the slightest trace since her temporary residence in the town. By heaven I would not for kingdoms exchange that graceful simplicity of hers, for the stiff and varnished exterior of art. I could not endure that my wife should mouth her sentiments, be demure in her smiles, studied in her manners, mincing in her gait. Let her be ever the original which nature has formed her; ever bearing the fresh unworn traces of her plastic hand—no breathing mummy, no mockery of her real self. All soul, all ardour, all enthusiasm ! You see in her countenance the thought of her mind ere she utters it. It would cost her more pain to disguise a single sentiment of her breast, than ever it cost a courtier to speak the truth.

Such as she is, may she, I fervently pray, ever remain. How will the soul of your Amelia greet her, each will read at once, as in a faithful mirror, the mind of the other! reciprocal love and esteem will spring up in their hearts—may their friendship be as warm, my Darlowitz, and last till the cessation of ours.

———

Yesterday Julia said to me, " I feel no regret at quitting this town, save one."

" And what is that?" inquired I.

" I think the Countess Zulmer a charming woman—do not you?" she added.

" She is very elegant and agreeable," I replied.

" Oh! and she is so amiable," cried Julia, with that vivacity she always displays when praising another—" she has so good a heart too"—

". I believe she has, Julia," answered I; " but why do you regret her, since she is far more calculated for the gay world than for retirement; believe me she would find no happiness in what is about to constitute ours."

" Do you think not," said Julia. " The Countess appears to have so much sensibility—I hope she will visit us sometimes."

" Possibly," I replied; " but when you are once acquainted with the Countess Darlowitz, I should be sorry to see you regret any other female. You will find in her every amiable quality you think you perceive in the Countess, and a thousand others which she does *not* possess."

" The poor Countess!" said Julia, " she had not an husband that loved her, neither had she ever any children to call forth her affections."

" I have always understood the Count Zulmer was infinitely attached to her—why else indeed should he have married her, since she had no riches to attract him."

" How fond she is of children," said Julia—" that is a proof of a good heart— Augustus is her favourite, for she says he is *so like you.* I cannot help loving the Countess, *if it were only for that.*"

What a creature, Darlowitz! this is the noble simplicity that enchants me; her heart and mind are so transcendently pure, that she has no thought of evil; the shadow of it could not glance across the polished surface of her spotless mind. Her affections, her whole soul, are so devoted to me, that she makes my breast her sanctuary, and she would easier believe this globe were motionless than that the idea of another could find entrance there.

Oh! thou fair image, which reignest despotic and triumphant in my heart! Well and truly dost thou judge me, and when another is for an instant admitted there, fly then for ever from that guilty heart, fly it—as unworthy longer to retain thee.

Thou knowest, my friend, and canst easily conceive, why I do not wish to converse with my innocent and charming wife upon the subject of the Countess Zulmer. I have never entered into any detail of my former acquaintance with that female, her expectations, or the consequent explanations I found myself called upon to make; partly from delicacy towards her, and partly from an unconquerable repugnance on my own side to revert to the topic. I clearly perceive the Countess herself has never given the smallest hint to Julia of past occurrences, either indirectly or otherwise; so far I must do justice to her sense of propriety and decorum, though probably I may owe more to her pride than to any thing else. Be the cause what it may, I am satisfied with the effect, and having different times given the matter every impartial consideration in my own mind, I have never yet convinced myself of the necessity or propriety of entering into an uninteresting detail to Julia of what does not, and never can, in any way concern her. It is true the Countess Zulmer condescended some years back to entertain favourable sentiments for me—but they were unknown to any but herself and me; no one suspected the preference she professed; how should they—when she appeared the same to all? Whatsoever she said, was said for the world, whatsoever she did was done for every one. Without the homage of the crowd she was lost. Why then should I stamp with consequence the ephemeral sentiments of such a woman by narrating to my wife a dull chain of past, almost forgotten events?

Yet, believing as I do, the Countess Zulmer to be a woman of strict unimpeachable virtue, and that her character is without stain, (for though she is admired, and by many of her sex envied, I never yet heard *that* questioned) I could have no hesitation in permitting her the society of my wife. At the same time I must confess, had not an undesired chance thrown her in our path on my return to Vienna, I certainly should not have sought her out for the mere purpose of introduction. Many reasons might have co-operated to deter me from that step, but it would have appeared singular, and have been at once ungenerous and imprudent to have obviously shunned her when accident had brought us together. And what excuse, what motive could I have assigned for doing so ? Her conduct is so truly unexceptionable, her manners so gentle and dignified, that the most querulous and fastidious critic could find no fault with her.

She appears to have wholly lost that vivaciousness, bordering on levity, for which she was once distinguished, but she has in fact lost nothing in point of real attraction. She has gained, on the contrary, for she inspires respect and interest, where before she excited only admiration—a sentiment which may be experienced at once with the profoundest indifference.

Oh ! if women did but know how much more pleasing to men of refinement, is delicacy and softness, than an exuberant gaiety, or even wit itself, how differently directed would be their exertions, how much lighter their labour. Nothing, in my mind, is so detestable in a woman, as obtrusive qualities. Men can never be *compelled* into admiration; they must be charmed—enticed into it. The homage of the soul is not to be gained by storm.

Yet how different Appollonia appears now, from what she did five or six years ago. How changed her manners—she is reserved, nay, sometimes melancholy—

or is it from the effect of extreme contrast
that I think her melancholy, when
she is only not gay. I have never heard
any one observe on this, to me, obvious
alteration in her, but it is no small mark of
the perverseness of our sex, that notwith-
standing she is now so much more worthy
of being admired than she was formerly,
she has fewer admirers and has not a single
lover that I have heard of. Instead of being
surrounded as before by a crowd of young
men, and the giddy and thoughtless of her
own sex, you now see conversing with
her, persons of understanding and virtue,
who appear to listen with pleasure to the
observations she makes. Formerly the
empty crowd stood round her, seeming to
have learned their task by rote, ready with
the servile bow for her self-arrogated
homage, or with the loud unmeaning
laugh for her flippant wit, her less elegant than ready repartee; or with the ful-
some compliment to fill up the vacant

moment. How different, how valuable, the real consideration she now meets with. She is admitted, nay courted, into the first and best societies. This might, with justice, be gratifying to her pride—the former, had she but reflected, must have humbled her in her own eyes; and, yet I repeat to thee, strange, yet true it is, amid all the approbation she merits and obtains—amid all the respect she excites, not a single lover is to be seen—not one bold enough to acknowledge himself a captive to real worth.

How is this? are those who used so unequivocally to profess their admiration for her afraid of the charge of inconsistency, by continuing their homage now? or, is it that they believe a reformed coquet is not to be seriously loved, and are afraid to encounter her, alluring as she appears? It is barely justice to the Countess to say, that her deportment

towards myself, and in my presence, is
the most delicate, the most correct and
dignified that it is possible to conceive.
She neither presumes on our former acquaintance to treat me with familiarity,
nor is she guilty of the odious affectation
of a sullen reserve, which would be still
worse from the allusion it would bear to
the past, and that it was remembered
with bitterness. She holds in her beha-
viour the due medium, she is cordially polite, and a stranger could surmise nothing
but that being on terms of the tenderest
friendship with the wife, she proportiona-
bly regarded the husband.

In truth she does appear infinitely to
admire, I had almost said, to love Julia.
To manifest such a disposition, the nature
must be excellent. I believe then, that
she feels for her sincere regard, and it is
clear that she has succeeded in inspiring
Julia with a reciprocal one.

I can surmise no possible motive that could induce Appollonia on this occasion to feign sentiments she did not feel; therefore I am the more inclined to give her credit for them, and particularly as I think they must be unusually proof against the impression of excellence, who could behold, and converse with Julia, and not admire and love her.

But leaving for the present a subject on which I have been involuntarily led to dwell thus long, let me inform thee, not without infinite regret, that our dear Rozendorf declines accompanying us to Lintz. He says that to live in the midst of a species of happiness, such as he can never hope to enjoy, otherwise than in the contemplation, would be too much for him.— "What!" said he to me, when I closely pressed him to join our society, "would be my fate, if at my time of day, irresistibly acquiring a taste for domestic de-

M 3

lights, I mean such as are attendant on the married life, I should gradually feel my isolated state becoming obnoxious to me, and view it with disgust? What if in useless regrets I wore out the wretched residue of my days? or worse, if chusing a wife, I provoked fortune to punish my tardiness, by cruel disappointment, and a long series of miseries now unknown to me? No, no, my dear Wiemar, let me remain as I am; at present I experience unalloyed happiness, in hearing of the happiness of those I love, and of occasionally beholding it. I feel not my solitary state, situated as I now am, but it may appear a solecism to say, that it would too forcibly present itself to me, if I lived in the midst of your united and numerous family. Residing in this great city, I see hundreds like myself; I mingle with society if I please, or if not I retire to my chamber in the company of some moral, refined or philosophical author, and the hours I thus consume in the silence of my study, are not the most unpleasant of my life. I fancy myself like Pliny, that is to say, in his solitude only, who praises in an epistle to Trajan, or one of his friends, the delightful retirement of his Laurentinum——the beauty of its situation, but above all, that he can be there silent, and removed from the voices of servants, and every other kind of disturbance. Add to all this, I possess two dear friends, in whose concerns I am strongly interested, and in whose felicity or sorrow I equally participate. Thus have I neither leisure nor inclination to observe, that I am merely a cypher in society. If I were taken out of my present routine, to which my mind is habituated, and to which long custom has perfectly reconciled me, you possibly might be one of the first to regret the consequences of such an act."

What think you, my dear Darlowitz?

I believe, indeed, that we shall better
evince our love for our friend, by permitting him to remain as he is, and to
do in all respects as he thinks fit—his
habits are invincible, and we could not
make him more happy—his mode of life
is regular, rational, and agreeable to his
feelings—why, if a man pursuing a certain path, finds it delightful and gratifying to his taste, and at the same time is
assured that it is not dangerous, should
over-officious friends seek forcibly to
drag him thence, by pointing out, or
telling him of one, which *they* conceive to
be more pleasant, more beautiful, but cannot affirm to be equally safe for him.—
Besides, alone as he appears to us, he is
surrounded as it were by a family of virtues—he is the friend of man—he is active in good, and though perhaps he may
not, like the Spartans, conceive the highest excellence to consist in presenting
children to the state, he has a thousand

other excellencies of greater value, morally speaking, to society.

Therefore let us consult his pleasure as
he has ever consulted ours, and abstain
from pressing him to that against which
he seems to have insurmountable objec-
tions. I must now conclude by entreat-
ing thee to take upon thyself the trouble
of seeking a suitable habitation for me and
mine. I should wish the house to be
spacious, but not unnecessarily so, and a
garden with some ground attached to
it. The situation as good as thou canst
select, but commanding, at all events, a
prospect of the mansion in which thou
dwellest, which will always appear to us
the sweetest feature in the landscape;
farewel: present to the Countess Darlowitz the best wishes of my Julia, and
myself, for the prolongation of her happiness and thine. Kiss all thy darlings

for me, but give more than one to thy eldest Frederick, my godson.

LETTER XXV.

THE COUNTESS DARLOWITZ TO THE DUCHESS DE STERNACH.

Lintz.

YES, my ever honored mother, in answer
to your dear letter,* I inform you that the
happiness of your daughter is as perfect
as that of mortal can or ought to be. My
Darlowitz is still the best of husbands, the
tenderest of fathers.

Since I made the determination of
quitting the gay world, and devoting my-

This letter does not appear.

self, jointly with him, to the education of our children, I have had no moment of vacancy, no cause for regret. As Heaven thought fit to bless me with a numerous family, I beheld increasing responsibility attaching to me in this life, and that to fulfil those responsibilities and render myself worthy of divine favour, I must resign myself to my duties.

The strongest resolution, living in the midst of the world, would have availed me little; and if I had been frequently obliged to quit my children, I must have trusted them in the power and to the example of mercenaries, who would have taught them purely for their own gratification, to indemnify themselves for my unwilling absence, by seeking new sources of entertainment, and having recourse, in all probability, to such means as would be most improper for them: thus, doubly corrupting their minds by causing them to indulge in what was in itself injurious and forbidden, and practising them early in deceit, falsehood, and disobedience. Besides which, I have always considered a too early introduction into promiscuous society, as detrimental rather than serviceable to youth. They must of necessity hear mixed conversation, variety of remark and observations, the purport and tendency of which, from not fully comprehending, they are liable to draw thence erroneous inferences and dangerous conclusions, such as not unfrequently tincture their ideas, and influence insensibly their conduct through life.

They must often, likewise, observe much which is ridiculous or improper, and so deep are the impressions of youth, that what was observed, and the idea produced at the moment, generally accompany each other to the latest period during which memory recals the circumstance.

According to my ideas, a parent is highly amenable for the moral character of their offspring. I will not enter into the philosophical question of how far *nature* is to be arraigned for certain tendencies of the disposition or propensities of the mind, but will only say, that I must consider a parent as solely amenable for such faults of the *character*, as due attention to a right system of education might (if not wholly have surmounted) at least have so attempered and ameliorated, as to blend without much ruggedness into the line of virtue.

But, that I might neither screen myself by throwing the blame on nature, nor yet let them run the hazard of being influenced by example, I determined to see the dispositions and ideas of my children unfold under my own eye, and to be guided in my conduct by what I should thus intimately observe of them ; for after all our rules and systems, *nature* should be strictly attended to, and consulted in our treatment of children. Why is it that so many arrive at maturity with bad dispositions, which never afterwards forsake them, but from this principle being too much neglected?

In short, for the purpose of performing my duty, I made a bold effort to escape from what are falsely called the *pleasures of life*. I had some little trouble to encounter, as you know, my dear mother, to induce the Count to come immediately into my plan, though ultimately I prevailed.—But what was the wonder? He was so young at the time; we had been married but four years; he was barely twenty six; it is now nearly eight since I carried my point. He was so admired, his company so courted, in truth I feared that his attention would be too much divided; nay, absolutely that it would be

residence you have chosen ? does the sea
air produce on you all the fine effects
which your doctors promised you should
experience ? If so, I will not ask you to
remove from its influence. Is not your
health more dear to me than my own
gratification ? What do I say ?—could I
derive gratification from any act of yours,
unconnected with your well-being ? Is
not my happiness inseparably linked with
your life and health ? Stay, then, my
dearest mother—stay where you are, if you
derive any benefit from so doing. I shall
be more happy than if you were with
me.

I must not conclude this letter without
informing you, that your favourite, the
Count Wiemar, arrived here about four
days ago, accompanied by his beautiful
wife and children, neither of whom till
then Darlowitz or myself had had the plea-
rure of beholding. On Count Wiemar it

is unnecessary for me to pass any other eulogium, than merely to say, that he is the same Wiemar we ever knew him. . I believe it is about five years since either of us saw him last. I can perceive no difference in him, unless it be that his countenance bears in it a stronger character of happiness, if I may be allowed the expression, than it did before. This is owing to his having espoused a woman whom he tenderly loves, and who has made him the proud father of two as beauteous children as my eyes ever beheld. Wiemar now experiences that species of happiness, for which I think he ever appeared to be particularly formed by nature—the happiness of being the chief of a family. How well does he support the character of a husband and a father! You would be delighted, my dear mother, could you see him. You, who always admired him, would now behold in him additional claims for admiration.—

Added to the same suavity of manners as ever, the same gentleness and mild dignity, there is such an interesting sense of bliss diffused throughout his air—such a love, such a joyous animation sparkles in his eyes, when he speaks of, or contemplates his wife and infants. The countenance of my Darlowitz, too, is lighted up with unusual pleasure at having once more near him, so dear a friend, and at beholding him in the possession of that felicity he has so often wished him.

As for the Countess Wiemar, it would be presumption in me yet to pass an opinion on her, but while my eyes bear testimony to her personal perfections, it is but natural for me to infer that her moral ones must correspond with them, to have attracted and rivetted the heart of a Wiemar. He is no common man, nor would, I am persuaded, a common-minded woman, however exquisite her beauty might be, have possessed any charms for him.

There is a somewhat extremely fascinating in the appearance and manners of the Countess Wiemar, which I think is chiefly attributable to a most engaging artlessness and simplicity, conspicuous in both. I understand that she has passed nearly the whole of her life in one of the most secluded spots in Switzerland, and that in consequence, she is to society, and its formal usages, almost a stranger. This accounts for the native grace, I have remarked in her, and it is impossible she could exchange it with advantage for any artificial polish which long residence in the society of what is called the great world, could bestow; for indeed what polish that art can give, can ever equal natural grace. Though nearly five years married, she is extremely young, and the sweet simplicity of her appearance, causes

her to seem even younger than she is.
I never saw a female so fair, so little indebted to studied dress or ornament;
you perceive at one view, that the embel-
lishment of her person forms no part of
her anxiety; her head has no decoration
but her luxuriant hair, her figure none
but the simplest white robe negligently
folded round her, neither aiming to reveal
her charms, nor affectedly concealing
them, but imparting to her person that
flowing grace which is so conspicuous
in the finest models of ancient sculp-
ture.

She interested me the moment I beheld
her, and in return for some little civility
of mine, on her first introduction to me
by her husband, she pressed the hand I
extended towards her, and with a vivacity
and energy that could not fail to flatter
me, she cried, " How happy am I, that I
at length behold the Countess Darlowitz,

of whom I have thought so much since Count Wiemar described to me her excellence; deign, madam, to favour me with your friendship, of which I shall strive to be worthy, and which will exalt me in my own eyes."

I returned the best answer I could to so obliging a compliment; and certainly I anticipate much pleasure from the cultivation of her acquaintance. With my children she appeared absolutely enraptured, and you will not wonder, my dear mother, if in the eyes of a fond parent she thus gained additional charms. She next presented to me her own, and seemed as anxious for my opinion of them, as if it could add to, or detract aught from their loveliness, or as if I were a judge about to pass sentence.

Darlowitz has been sufficiently fortunate to procure for his friend and charming family, a habitation very little removed from our own, and abounding with every internal convenience, and beauty of prospect and scenery without. As soon as it can be got in perfect readiness for their reception, they will take possession of it; this a few days will accomplish—till when they are our guests. The Countess Wiemar professes herself delighted at this, because it will give her, she says, an opportunity of studying me in every situation, each hour of the day; she will then see how I portion my time, and what are my plans, and be enabled to form herself, as she too-flatteringly expresses it, upon so perfect a model.

Indeed, my dear mother, this fair stranger honours me more than I merit, but her diffidence (always a proof of extraordinary merit) will not permit her to entertain the smallest idea of her own perfections.   Alas! what am I, that any one should bow down to me?   what do I more than barely fulfil the *duties* which Providence has allotted me on earth?   If I did less—if I neglected them, I must be criminal.   I have no claim, then, but to the praise of negative virtue.   I am in the commission of no positive good, I am simply, not evil.

Adieu, my dearest mother; whatsoever I may be, one feeling must ever reign paramount in my breast—the tenderes treverence for you, who are indeed all virtue. ——Count Wiemar anxiously inquired concerning you; he entreats me to tender you his most ardent wishes for your happiness and perfect recovery of your health. Darlowitz begs I may not forget him in my letter. Once more adieu, my mother.

LETTER XXVI.

THE DUCHESS DE STERNACH TO HER DAUGHTER.

Naples.

HOW pleasing to me, my beloved child, the praise you ascribe to me. How delightful is it to me to trace that dear hand in the expression of such sentiments: My heart expands with gratitude to the God of heaven for having blessed me with such a daughter. Why do you detract from your intrinsic virtue, and endeavour to philosophize it away? Is it then nothing, in the bloom of life to have resigned the world and all its pleasures, so highly, though unjustly appreciated by the aggregate of mankind, particularly by those whom age and experience have not yet rendered callous to their allurements? Is it nothing, with the fortitude of a heroine to have slighted these, and to have devoted yourself to almost monastic seclusion for the welfare of your children ? If the climax of virtue consists in living for others rather than ourselves, in sacrificing our pleasures to their advantage, in resigning ourselves up, heart and soul, to the most undeviating performance of our duties, in pointing out the path to heaven through good acts to our children, and perfecting their souls for immortality, then have you attained this climax, and arrived as near perfection as mortal can. May your earthly reward, my dear Amelia, be, that your children may repay your care as you have repaid mine.

I am pleased to learn that you have received so agreeable an addition to your little society. Amiable Wiemar, no felicity can be too great for him ; if he hath chosen a wife worthy of himself, she must, indeed, possess every good quality. I perceive in her already an irrefragable proof of excellence—it is that she has selected you for her model. Your united families, removed from the great world, will form a little world of themselves. Your husband will have with him the friend of his early youth, whom most he loves and honours, and you need not, I think, entertain the apprehension that, surrounded and embosomed by all he holds dear on the earth, he can ever desire to mingle again with the idle and vacant throng.

You will have no cause, I think, to regret the introduction of this little family to yours. There are many moments, I had almost said hours, which, from the nature of your avocations with your younger children, you must necessarily pass away from your husband, and though I know the rich stores and fine resource he possesses in his own mind, and tha he is, when alone, never unemployed, yet believe me, the company of a much loved friend will frequently be no unpleasing substitute for solitary reflection, or for a book, however edifying.

The society of an agreeable interesting female companion will beguile much of your own leisure too, which you will pass with increased pleasure, and your little ones will not be the worse for mingling with other children of dispositions equally good with their own. I wish, indeed, my dearest Amelia, I could be among you all, but my health will not, I fear, permit my removing for long. The delicious atmosphere of this place agrees with me so well, I seem already to have gained ten years to my life. The street in which I reside lies open to the bay, my windows look immediately upon the sea, and when I rise in the morning my first step is to throw them up and let down the blinds, by which means I at once enjoy the salt breeze and exclude the ardent beams of the sun. The windows are very well fenced with the blinds and light curtains, or there would be no living for the intense heats during the day. But an hour before sun-rise, and after it has set, no language can convey to you an idea of the balmy freshness and fragrance which is to be enjoyed by stepping into my balcony, which juts out over the sea.

You know, my dear child, I must consider myself a native of Idalia, inasmuch as I was born in this country, though not of Italian parents. Afterwards, you have heard me say, I received great part of my education in a convent here, and hence I verily believe my constitution became so imbued with the climate that no other would ever afterwards agree with me equally well. I cannot say I ever enjoyed pefect health in any country but this, and

I must consider that my physicians judged rightly in prescribing me to return hither as to my native air.

If it were not for your numerous family I should venture to express a hope, that were my residence here to continue for a very long period, it would not wholly pass without a visit from you 'and your husband; but on this too pleasing thought I must not dare to dwell, contenting myself for the present with having merely breathed it.

How would your refined and elegant mind be gratified, my child, at beholding yourself on classic ground, and viewing with pleasing awe some of those sublime vestiges of antiquity, the bare description of which used to afford you so much delight. What emotions would be excited in your soul when you reflected on the nothingness of human grandeur—the fragility, compared with time, of the most stupendous labours of man. How long the monuments of his pomp and vanity endure beyond himself, yet at length moulder like him into decay. His sumptuous palaces, his walls of marble and his gates of brass; his collossal statues, his lofty pillars of granite, or of the hardest adamant, all yielding to the conquering hand of Time, and what he meant to perpetuate his name, perpetuating along with it the memory of his pride and weakness! But you, indeed, need not these local testimonies to exalt or add sublimity to your reflections, you already duly appreciate the things of this earth, and found your fame, your *immortal* fame, on a life of virtue alone. May heaven bless you and yours, and continue you long the glory and happiness of your husband and children.

LETTER XXVII.

APPOLLONIA ZULMER TO MADAME DE HAUTVILLE.

Vienna.

COUNT Wiemar has left Vienna, and what is worse, he has taken his wife with him. I am in despair—did I say despair! I retract the word, for what, that mortal can do shall make me despair? Appollonia is not to be thus foiled, when resolved on taking her just revenge! No, no, poor Wiemar, thy petty efforts and artifices, what are they but as the flutterings of a bird in the inextricable net, all tending the more to entangle him.

Dost thou presume to think, poor presumptuous creature as thou art! that thou canst escape for ever unpunished for the

outrages thou hast committed ?—for the
double outrage, first, by rejecting me
with scorn, but not content with the rash
provocation thus given me, by further
daring to appear before me with thy
wedded wife !- -the woman thus avowedly
preferred to me. And didst thou truly in
thy heart believe that all this I should see,
and suffer tamely?—Gentle Wiemar! thou
judgest by thyself, I presume, in thy for-
giveness and forgetfulness of injuries.
It is true, from that fatal night on which
I was rejected by thee, I hated thee as
Satan hated the inmates of Paradise,
and with as much eagerness and rage
planned thy destruction. I had none to
assist my councils ; in my own soul I
vowed unpitying vengeance against thee,
and to persecute thee through life. Ah !
how I laughed at thee, when, coward as
thou wert, thou soughtest safety, in flight,
as if time or absence could quench in
my breast the inextinguishable spark

which blazed there, vivid and fierce for thee !

I might not probably have taken on thee such signal and dreadful vengeance as it is now my intention to take, hadst thou not, by this second insult crowning the first, urged me to it ; but whatever thy crimes, thy punishment shall be pro-portionate—like Satan will I aim it, not direct at thee, but thine. Delusion shall entice the woman, and ruin be hurled upon the man.——Again hast thou fled, to elude me probably; in vain—my in-fluence pursues thee still ! I am as a powerful enchantress who permits her spell-bound victims to rove in illusory li-berty, yet whom her charms ever sur-rounding, she can at any time compel into her presence.

I must own, indeed, that the spot thou hast selected for thy wanderings is not the most favourable for my incantations, but that my power can easily overcome, for what are the localities of time or place to one whose spells can reach the heart and govern the understanding? The *presence of the* person is unnecessary—mere matter, and but a gross drug in the sublimated system of my proceedings. My aim is the empire of the mind and soul— the jewel which is within the casket. Have you never marked the progress of the canker in the rose? the worm touches its heart, and it falls—its beauty is soon perished and gone! Can you not draw the inference? If you cannot, wait patiently till time explains it to you.

You admit that I have suffered the deepest injury that woman can sustain— yet you would have me with stoic indifference—even with the remembrance of insult—the keen sense of degradation still rankling at my heart, dismiss all thoughts of vengeance—give contempt for contempt, and, like a soulless wretch seek still the gross pleasures of life, insensible to the abasements I may meet with in the pursuit.—No! unfortunately I have a soul! a soul too keenly susceptible, actuated by the profoundest emotions—capable of the most devoted attachment, yet tremblingly alive to unmerited insult. I have no lukewarm sentiments, my feelings are passions, and I must adore, or detest!

Would Wiemar have loved me, but for a single year, I would have sold myself to destruction for the luxurious bliss!—but he has hated and rejected me, so will I now equally sell myself to destruction to destroy him. How dare he imagine that he shall lead a life of unbroken joy with another, while I, sick with envy and jealous rage, look on and writhe in tortures, for which language can find no name. Toppled from my high eminence, I will not singly fall, others shall be dragged down, and struggle with me in the depths of my despair.

How wisely (as he thinks) judged the haughty Wiemar, when he presumed to believe that by conveying his wife beyond the verge of my immediate presence, he conveyed her likewise beyond the verge of my power. His vanity and presumption he shall dearly rue. And Julia! ungrateful as she is—yes, ungrateful, for as she can neither see the emotions which sway my heart, nor suspect the plans I have in view, she has no reason but to believe in the sincerity of my regard—she, influenced no doubt by her lordly husband, has never once written to me since her departure.

But, oh! how feeble these barricadoes against *me*. Subtle as air, I enter in all directions—irresistibly and invisibly sur-rounding them. Sagacious Wiemar! could I not, if I chose, openly pursue you? The city of Lintz is no territory of yours. I too, if I chose, might in common with many others, select some spot there to retire to.—I know several families near the very place they have selected, who would rejoice in any opportunity that should afford them a visit from me ;— but no, no, I shall not have recourse to this measure, it is unnecessary for me.

I know the simple Julia—I have studied her; she is pleased with me, nay, more, without vanity I may say I possess her friendship. Tis true, indeed, I have known her but a year ; yet with attentive management how much may be accomplished, and what progress may not be made on an unsuspecting nature in a much less period. I consider a grand desideratum obtained, in having gained her confidence, and really I do not believe, (but conscience you know leads us to suspect strange things) I do not believe, dispassionately speaking, that Wiemar has any aversion to me. I know, good creature! he entertains a high opinion of my heart and understanding, yet feeling myself how much cause he has to hate and spurn me, I instinctively conclude he does both; just as if, (which the powers forbid) I had a window in my breast, betraying the movements within.

Adieu, my dear preceptress—I have promised to confide to you every step. You, remote from the crowd, are the only real friend I can reckon on upon earth, and when I reveal to you my sentiments, intentions, and the secret emotions which rack my troubled soul, I seem but reflecting with, or uttering my thoughts to myself.

I had almost forgotten to tell you, that

my vile earthly plagues, Pietro Mondovi
and Catherine Glatz, are eternally re-
quiring somewhat or other at my hands,
to repay the dear bought service I was so
unhappy as to owe them—service which it
cost them nothing to render, but for which,
it should seem, I can never sufficiently
repay them. It would be easier to ap-
pease the hungry tigers of the desert,
than the insatiable rapacity of these
wretches. Sullen and refractory, they
are the petty torments that fill up the few
moments when my mind would emerge
from more racking anguish—and how *can*
I pacify them? I own to you, that the
folly, the madness if you will, which you
have so often reprobated, still keeps me
poor. But I have too much leisure on my
hands now; it will not be always thus,
and then other pursuits will cause
this tempting hazardous mischief to
lose its attraction in my eyes. Mean-
time, I entreat you write answers to

the letters I inclose,* and obtain if possible some little respite for me from their
merciless persecutions—as to myself, I am
weary—would the earth would swallow
them.   Once more, adieu!

---

* These letters not being material, do not appear.

END OF VOL. I.

J. M'Creery, Printer,
Black-Horse-Court, Fleet-Street,
London.

GOTHIC NOVELS

An Arno Press Collection

Series I

Dacre, Charlotte ("Rosa Matilda"). **Confessions of the Nun of St. Omer,** A Tale. 2 vols. 1805. New Introduction by Devendra P. Varma.

Godwin, William. **St. Leon:** A Tale of the Sixteenth Century. 1831. New Foreword by Devendra P. Varma. New Introduction by Juliet Beckett.

Lee, Sophia. **The Recess:** Or, A Tale of Other Times. 3 vols. 1783. New Foreword by J. M. S. Tompkins. New Introduction by Devendra P. Varma.

Lewis, M[atthew] G[regory], trans. **The Bravo of Venice,** A Romance. 1805. New Introduction by Devendra P. Varma.

Prest, Thomas Preskett. **Varney the Vampire.** 3 vols. 1847. New Foreword by Robert Bloch. New Introduction by Devendra P. Varma.

Radcliffe, Ann. **The Castles of Athlin and Dunbayne:** A Highland Story. 1821. New Foreword by Frederick Shroyer.

Radcliffe, Ann. **Gaston De Blondeville.** 2 vols. 1826. New Introduction by Devendra P. Varma.

Radcliffe, Ann. **A Sicilian Romance.** 1821. New Foreword by Howard Mumford Jones. New Introduction by Devendra P. Varma.

Radcliffe, Mary-Anne. **Manfroné:** Or The One-Handed Monk. 2 vols. 1828. New Foreword by Devendra P. Varma. New Introduction by Coral Ann Howells.

Sleath, Eleanor. **The Nocturnal Minstrel.** 1810. New Introduction by Devendra P. Varma.

Series II

Dacre, Charlotte ("Rosa Matilda"). **The Libertine.** 4 vols. 1807.
New Foreword by John Garrett. New Introduction by
Devendra P. Varma.

Dacre, Charlotte ("Rosa Matilda"). **The Passions.** 4 vols. 1811.
New Foreword by Sandra Knight-Roth. New Introduction
by Devendra P. Varma.

Dacre, Charlotte ("Rosa Matilda"). **Zofloya;** Or, The Moor:
A Romance of the Fifteenth Century. 3 vols. 1806. New
Foreword by G. Wilson Knight. New Introduction by
Devendra P. Varma.

Ireland, W[illiam] H[enry]. **The Abbess,** A Romance. 4 vols.
1799. New Foreword by Devendra P. Varma. New
Introduction by Benjamin Franklin Fisher IV.

[Leland, Thomas]. **Longsword,** Earl of Salisbury: An
Historical Romance. 2 vols. 1775. New Foreword by
Devendra P. Varma. New Introduction by Robert D. Hume.

[Maturin, Charles Robert]. **The Albigenses:** A Romance.
4 vols. 1824. New Foreword by James Gray. New
Introduction by Dale Kramer.

Maturin, Charles Robert ("Dennis Jasper Murphy"). **The Fatal
Revenge:** Or, The Family of Montorio. A Romance.
3 vols. 1807. New Foreword by Henry D. Hicks. New
Introduction by Maurice Lévy.

[Moore, George]. **Grasville Abbey:** A Romance. 3 vols. 1797.
New Foreword by Devendra P. Varma. New Introduction
by Robert D. Mayo.

Radcliffe, Ann. **The Romance of the Forest:** Interspersed With
Some Pieces of Poetry. 3 vols. 1827. New Foreword by
Frederick Garber. New Introduction by Devendra P.
Varma.

[Warner, Richard]. **Netley Abbey:** A Gothic Story. 2 vols.
1795. New Introduction by Devendra P. Varma.